Fractal

DANIEL JAWS

Printed in the United States of America

Published September 2025

Published by:
Between Friends Publishing, LLC
1080 SR 96,
Suite #100,
Warner Robins, GA 31088

ISBN: 978-1-956544-72-5

For my Goddess

CHAPTER 1
LASSIA

Fiery trails fill the night sky with scars. Blazing down from an unknown place, a giant ball of fire and smoke barrels down towards the ground. The intensity of the flames is so great that you could see it from anywhere on Erythem, the only habitable continent on this planet. Lassia is stargazing from her hammock. It is placed perfectly, surrounded by trees with the most stunning view of the sky above the canopies. When the object appears, she leaps out of her suspended paradise and sprints to her room for a better look. Lassia lives in a naturalistic fortress of sorts. The structures are covered in vines with blooming flowers and shining gemstones. Hidden away in the most magical forest in all of Erythem, it is a highly powerful place that is reserved for royalty. She rummages through her storage chest, looking for her spyglass. *Where is this bitch?*

She lets out a big sigh of relief when she finally has it in her grasp. She runs to her balcony and it doesn't take much to find her objective. It is still visible from her high vantage point. She points her spyglass and does her best to focus on what is beyond the smoke and flames. *No fucking way!*

It is a Super Seven gemstone, a combination of seven minerals (Amethyst, Clear Quartz, Smoky Quartz, Cacoxenite, Rutile, Goethite, and Lepidocrocite) found in one crystal, believed to possess powerful spiritual and healing properties. That's a Sacred Seven. The last Super Seven, or Sacred Seven as known by the people of Erythem, was last seen over one hundred years ago. No one knew how or why it disappeared, but one day it was simply gone. Lassia knows the magnitude of the appearance of such an important gemstone. She has to share the news with the ruler of her homeland Idyll, the Goddess Elina, who just so happened to be her stepmother.

Lassia was a human princess that was well known for her incredible healing abilities. Abilities that almost rivaled her beauty. She had long, dirty blonde hair and a body with curves that were small but proportionate. Her delicate, white skin glows in the sunlight. There was a rumor that even the slightest glance from her would make you go mad. She has deep blue eyes with a white halo around them. The only woman said to be more alluring was the Goddess. Lassia was aware of her beauty but never flaunted it as her stepmother did. As she approaches her stepmother's bedroom door, she hears muffled voices and strange sounds emanating from the room. Carefully, she opens the door to see her stepmother laying naked on her bed surrounded by her servants.

The Goddess has four faithful servants that functioned as her bodyguards, butlers, and lovers. Their names are Agate, Hematite, Labradorite, and Tiger's Eye. It is their job to tend to every whim she has. Lassia always knew her stepmother was intimate with her servants, but had never witnessed it with her own eyes. She steadies herself at the doorway in silence, unsure how to proceed. *I should come back later, but I can't stop watching.*

Tiger's Eye, commonly referred to as "Tee," is the Goddess' hand. He is also the only orc. He's sitting at the foot of the bed, giving direction to the others. "Hem, eat her pussy like your next meal depends on it. Agate, suck on her nipples. Don't be shy with your teeth this time. Lab, pull your cock out and let our Goddess have an appetizer."

Tee is a master when it comes to Elina's pleasures and desires. He has spent most of his life as her right hand man. Servitude was optional and considered a great honor in Idyll. *Fuck that looks fun.* Lassia starts feeling a warmth between her legs. There is a wet spot forming on her silk thong.

"That's enough fluff, boys. It's time to fill all her holes," Tee says.

Agate unsheathes his cock and begins to stroke his length as Hem is already positioning himself underneath Elina.

"I hope you boys saved all your seed for me. I am feeling extra needy tonight," the Goddess utters to her sexual vessels.

Lab repositions himself between her legs and lines the tip of his wet cock with her pulsing opening. She moves her body in a serpentine way, craving what is about to penetrate her. Tee is standing beside the bed now, towering over Elina, with his hands placed on her neck. Hem and Lab look at each other as they get into their final positions. Then, with a synchronized nod, they enter her at the same time. Hem and Lab are deep in her pussy. They have perfect rhythm as they thrust in unison.

"Oh, fuck yes!" she growls.

"You love it when the boys stretch you out, don't you?" Tee mutters only inches from her face with his hands still firmly around her neck.

Elina lets out more moans and gasps of pleasure as she is getting beautifully fucked by such physical specimens.

"Shut her up!" Tee snarls at Agate who has been stroking for almost a minute.

A respectful nod comes from Agate as he plunges his length down the Goddess' throat. She gags for a moment, but powers through as he continues his deep sustained thrust down her throat. After a few seconds, she can't hold her breath any longer and slaps his muscled butt cheek. That's her favorite way to let the boys know she needs them to pull back. Agate removes his cock with a large string of deep throat saliva hanging from the tip.

"Again!" Tee commands.

The willing servant does as he is told. This time he does a more rapid thrusting, going in and out with the occasional deep throat hold. Elina is handling all these men like a champ! Lassia is starting to realize just how innocent her own sex life is.

"I need you inside me Tee!" Elina vocalizes, while holding Agate's cock in her right hand.

"As you wish, Goddess," he acknowledges her desires.

He pushes Lab out of the way and pulls out his oversized cock.

No fucking way that's going to fit.

"Find work elsewhere. It's my turn to worship," Tee growls. Hem removes his throbbing cock from Elina's opening and shifts it to a wanting hole, her butthole.

"That's a good boy, Hem," she moans as he enters her welcoming back door entrance.

Lab is moving over to her left side to give her two cocks to lick and suck at her leisure. Tee grabs his cock and begins to brush her pussy in an up and down motion, coating himself with her wetness. He licks his thumb and rubs her clit. She arches her back in preparation for his entrance. Even the two cocks she had inside her before were not enough to prepare her for Tee's full size.

"Stop teasing me, Tee! Fuck me!" she growls.

He begins his slow, intentional insertion. She gasps with a slight hitch in her voice. The massive pressure his cock is creating is causing Hem to have an even tighter fit in her asshole. He only gets a few more pumps before pulling out and exploding all over Elina and himself. Lab sees Hem cumming and that pushes him over the edge, he cums all over the Goddess' chest. Now it's just Tee in her pussy and Agate getting the soul sucked out of him. Lab walks over and starts kissing Agate while Hem helps suck his cock. Agate can't take it and cums all over Elina and Hem's faces. Tee is still steadily thrusting.

What the fuck is happening now?!

"Cum for me, Daddy," Elina says in a moan. She knows exactly what makes him tick. "I want your cum all over my perfect body. Cum for me."

Tee quickens his thrusts. Pressure is building. His balls are pulling up into his chiseled body. The veins all over his dark, tanned body become more and more visible.

"You are pure perfection, Elina," Tee whispers.

He is the only person, aside from Lassia, that has the privilege of calling the Goddess by her first name.

"Cum for me, now!" the Goddess commands in a louder volume than before.

Tee gives two hard and intentional thrusts before pulling his member out of her and unleashing ropes of cum all over her. His roar while he cums is loud enough to shake the chambers they were currently in.

Holy shit, that's a lot of cum!

"That's a good boy, Tee. I love being covered in your seed," Elina whimpers.

Tee is panting, trying to gather himself after such a powerful release. All the boys begin to clean up their sexual mess and prepare a bath for the Goddess.

"You can stop hiding, Lassia. I hope you enjoyed the show," Elina says as she steps into her warm bath.

Lassia fumbles into the room, not realizing she was not as stealthy as she imagined. "I..I'm sorry. I didn't mean to sneak. I was stuck."

"It's fine. Just a little midnight snack. What can I do for you, Lass?" Elina asks.

"Oh…right! I almost forgot why I came here in the first place," Lassia chuckles nervously. "A Sacred Seven just fell from the sky."

Elina let out a loud laugh. "How did you come across this information?"

"I saw it with my own eyes, like thirty minutes ago. That's why I came here," Lassia explains.

"Are you telling me that you have known about this the whole time? Why didn't you tell me sooner?" Elina demands.

"You had your hands full…and other things…literally," Lassia sputters.

"No time for jokes, girl! We need to send men to secure the crash site before those assholes from Ferric try to steal it for themselves. We cannot let them get a hold of the Sacred Seven!" Elina yells.

"Please, can I go? You know I am the best healer and I just recently cleansed and charged my malachite stone," Lassia whines.

Gemstones were the source of power for any who wielded them. These were mined by orcs and refined by humans. The peaceful cohabitation was established over two hundred years ago when humans fled their homeland of Melan due to a widespread illness. It was the orcs that saved them by showing humans the power of gemstones. In true human fashion, it took no time to exploit every different kind of gemstone for their properties and powers. Many civil wars broke out as a result. After fifty years of conflict, the continent was split into North and South lands, Ferric and Idyll, respectively. In Idyll, gemstones are given to royalty and individuals that hold specific positions in the hierarchy. In Ferric, gemstones are owned by those that are powerful enough to take it in whatever way they deem necessary. The northern lands were widely considered to be outlawed and full of thieves, murderers and hooligans; humans and orcs alike.

Like any source of power, gemstones need to be cleansed and charged to meet their full potential. Placing your gemstone in a bowl of dry sea salt or in a bowl of raw milk, honey and pure water will cleanse negative energy. The light of a full moon will charge it after a few hours. Lassia always took great care in keeping her malachite stone at its maximum potential.

Healers were given malachite to help channel healing abilities, as well as spiritual attunement. There are only four healers in all of Idyll and Lassia is the best. She quickly surpassed her mentor, Nemar, after just two years of pupilship. Her purity and natural talent were always the key characteristics Nemar pointed out during his mentorship.

"You are too valuable to me here. I promise you can go on the next quest. Which direction did this Sacred Seven fall towards?" Elina explains.

"Directly North of the courtyard," Lassia describes.

"Shit! That means it may be in the midlands. Tee, get an Aventurine fellowship prepared for departure at first light. Hem, spread news of the quest to the villagers to avoid panic," Elina directs.

Tee nods and exits the room.

This is bullshit. I should be going on this quest.

Elina gets out of the bath and is immediately covered by Hem with a towel. Agate and Lab were off to the side preparing her robe and some herbal tea.

"I want you to brief the Aventurine fellowship on what you saw and give them direction. Then meet me for brunch. I have a feeling I will wake up late and very hungry," Elina commands.

The boys look at each other with a devilish grin. Lassia scoffs and heads back to her own chambers.

CHAPTER 2
KYSIUS

There is a lot of commotion in the town tonight. What is all the fuss? Kysius is on his third mead of the night, trying to drown out the bad taste of the ungodly woman he just fucked. *Pussy is not pussy, do better man.* He takes another hard swig of his mead, slamming down the mug as he finishes the last bit. "Another one, Bron. I still taste her on my teeth."

"I told you not to fuck that orc chick. Humans have the best pussy," Bron snears.

"She gave good head though!" Kysius smirks through his forced chuckle.

"You need to fix yours, brother," Bron continues.

Kysius scoffs and welcomes his new mead with a thirsty smile. He frequented this bar for two reasons; his best friend is the bartender and no one cared he was a prince. It may be a small rusty outdoor bar, but it's his spot. This is the only place he could be treated normal-ish.

"Kysius, you need to look at this," Bron urges Kysius as he points at the night sky.

Fuck, are we going to die? Kysius jumps off his stool and stumbles out from under the bar's overhang. He gets a better look at what seems like the start of a big bang extinction.

"What do you reckon it is?" he asks Bron.

"Looks like a meteor," Bron replies.

"That's too shiny to be a plain old space rock, dude," Kysius counters.

"Hah! It's probably a Sacred then… loser," Bron jokes.

"Actually…you might be right, dumbass," Kysius laughs.

Bron's jaw dropped. Kysius is a well-educated orc prince, albeit still an asshole, who knew all there is to know about gemstones and their capabilities. He is also the leader of the Ferric Guard. His father, Thrasus, made sure to train his son in both academics and combat. The product is the perfect orc for any environment or situation. After all, this is the land where people take gemstones by any means. Kysius has no intention of ever giving up his tourmaline. It was given to him as a source of confidence, grounding and channeling negative energy. His mother was raped and murdered by some traders from Idyll. The hatred and rage that courses through his veins anytime he sees or hears someone from Idyll is uncontrollable. His tourmaline is the perfect stone for Kysius, as he knows how to store and utilize the energy to its maximum capacity.

"I need to go. I bet the old man is already losing his fucking mind," Kysius explains.

"Hey! You gonna pay your tab or...? Aaand he's gone. I guess I'll go fuck myself," Bron sighs.

It was not unusual for Kysius to forget to pay his tab. Bron knew he would pay him back, eventually. Bron is a long, dark haired human that is almost as tall as his orc friend. Orcs normally stood at six foot five inches, and that's just the average. He had green eyes and an athletic build. Women, both human and orc, were constantly fawning over him. However, his sights were set on something else. Something much more difficult to attain. He often wondered if it would ever be attainable.

Kysius made his way to the King's Hall. He approaches the massive double doors. Despite each door weighing over a hundred pounds, he opens them both with ease. They swing open and slam into the walls behind him with a thud. He stops halfway to the throne. A ray of moonlight with a splash of fiery red, from the Sacred, shined on him. He is one of the more muscular orcs in Ferric, as well as being the most handsome. His mother was human, making him a hybrid. He is the only one to ever survive. All other hybrids died within hours of birth. With his human-like face and orcish body, he is quite the sight. His skin is beige with shoulder length, black hair that he keeps in a ponytail. Posture and walking style leaning more towards his human side, being more upright than orcs.

"Father, have you noticed the sky tonight? It looks strange, huh?" Kysius asks. Kysius looks up at the windows that line the right wall. Thrasus looks down at his son with a disappointed look. "Kysius, why do you have to be a smart ass all the time?" Thrasus sighs.

Kysius shrugs his shoulders. "I'm just having a bit of fun before you send me off on a long quest to retrieve that Sacred."

"I should've known you would already know what it was," Thrasus retorts.

"You trained me well, Paapaa," Kysius says with a comedic tone.

Thrasus furrows his brows. "Don't call me that. It's weird."

"Sorry, Papi," Kysius teases.

"Kysius!" Thrasus snaps.

"Okay, Daddy, I will stop," Kysius says in a girly voice.

"Fuck off, Ky…" Thrasus says while unable to contain his laughter.

"Alright, alright, when do I leave for this mission?" Kysius asks.

"You will take a group of mercenaries to the crash site and bring me that Sacred. Leave as soon as you have the men and supplies you need," Thrasus directs.

Kysius turns and makes his exit. *Fuck, I didn't pay my tab…again.* A mixed group of humans and orcs are assembled at the front gate. Word must've gotten out fast. Kysius lifts up his hand to grab the mobs attention before addressing them. "Hello, everyone. I am in need of a few mercenaries. Have you guys seen any?"

Some scattered laughs and grunts come from the crowd gathered around him.

"Aye, we are all mercenaries here," says a younger looking orc in the front row.

Kysius looks at the boy with a furrowed brow. "Well, aren't you a cute little merc," he says with a mocking smile.

"Go fuck yourself! I will eat you for breakfast!" the youngling barks.

Kysius takes a step back and hold his hand over his heart. "Whoa! Someone should have cum on a rag…Fuck me." He turns his attention to the rest of the crowd that is filled with all kinds of criminals and outlaws. "I need a healer, gemologist and some strong backs to carry a heavy rock."

A few of the stronger looking orcs and humans stand out and Kysius motions them to come forward. "You guys will do. Now I just need a healer and gemologist."

An older human gentleman says he can do both.

"Great! Two birds, one stone. What's your name, old man?" Ky asks.

"Espacio, sir," the elderly man responds.

"I like your style," Ky adds.

With his party assembled, Kysius turns his attention to supplies and goodbyes. Going on quests is a common occurrence for him. It was an integral part of his training and growth, and still is. He had it down to a routine. Stop by the armory for weapons, then his room for supplies, then one last drink with his best friend. A few hours went by and everything was ready, bar one drink.

"Hey brother, it's that time again," Ky says.

"Final suck?" Bron asks.

"Final suck!" Ky repeats, referring to the crude nickname for his routine drink.

Bron slides a mug over to Kysius while pouring another drink.

"Oh shit, are you having it with me this time?" Ky asks.

"Yea, I'm feeling a bit zesty this morning," Bron replies.

"I fucking love it!" Ky shouts.

They raise their mugs. Bron never letting his eyes fall from Kysius' lips. "Cheers, bitch! Don't die out there."

"You know I can't die until I fuck your mom," Kysius replies with a raised eyebrow.

"You will never fuck my mom. She doesn't like your kind," Bron says while making a grossed out face.

"Mama Bron doesn't like orcs?" Kysius questions with a confused look.

"She loves orcs. She doesn't like little dick assholes that don't pay their bar tabs," Bron says with a playful smile and raised brow.

"Fair. A guy can dream though," Kysius sighs with a shrug.

They chug their mead and slam the mugs on the bar. They hold each other's gaze for a moment. They share a quiet moment of appreciation and understanding of what this could be. One of the mercenaries appears and taps Kysius' shoulder, breaking the trance. It was time to go. Bron watches as his friend moves over to his horse and mounts it. Their eyes meet one last time as they share a nod. Only a few moments pass as Kysius and his party of mercenaries fade into the distance.

chapter 3
LASSIA

The sky is full of smoke and embers from the falling gemstone. People all over the continent are in unrest. Lassia gathers some clothes and healing supplies. She is determined to join the Aventurine party. *I'm a grown ass woman! I do whatever the fuck I want.* Once she has her bag packed, she sprints downstairs to intercept Tee.

"Tee, wait up!" she says out of breath from running down the stairs.

"How can I help you, Lassia?" he asks with a raised brow.

"You need to let me be the healer for this party. She treats me like a child. I am twenty-five, for fuck's sake!" Lassia exclaims.

"And how, exactly, shall I tell her that I let her daughter go on a quest after she was strictly prohibited?" his brow raised even more.

"STEP daughter! Don't tell her I went. I will leave a note saying I went on a spiritual retreat," Lassia outlines.

"You want me to lie to the Goddess?" his face seemingly displeased.

"It's not a lie. This quest is basically a spiritual retreat," she says while rolling her eyes.

"What do I get if I conveniently forget about this conversation?" Tee asks.

"I will buy that necklace that you have been eyeballing for weeks," she says while sporting a cocky grin.

"What?! How do you even know about that?" he says in disbelief.

"I see you pass by that vendor almost every day. Why don't you buy it? I know who it's for," Lassia smirks. She punches his shoulder, making him crack a smile. Tiger's Eye had been in love with the Goddess for years. Seemingly, everyone but her notices that his devotion goes beyond duty.

"You know I cannot be seen buying a gift for the Goddess. It would put her in danger. We can't have that," Tee explains.

"Perfect! I mean…you know what I mean. I will get the necklace for you and you play dumb," Lassia plots. Lassia had a huge smile and positioned her hands as if to pray. Tee rolls his eyes and lazily nods. Her small and delicate hand extends towards his massive orcish chest, only to be met by his oversized hand. They shook and went about their business.

There is a group of twenty soldiers, two gemologists and four miners gathered around the courtyard. Tee stands on a platform used for performances during solstice. He addressed the gaggle of orcs and humans with a brief description of what the Goddess expected from this quest. An audible gasp came from all who were present, as Tee mentions that it is no ordinary quest. It is a quest for a Super Seven, the long awaited Sacred Seven. He quiets the crowd and finishes his briefing. "If there are no questions, may the diamond protect you," Tee concludes.

The diamond is the most powerful gemstone in all of Idyll. It conveys purity, love, success, strength, protection, and courage. This specific diamond is a large six-foot chunk that is kept in the center of the courtyard. There is a force-field around it that keeps out anyone that doesn't have a fractal. To receive a fractal of the diamond, you must have a current fractal holder grant you entrance. The only person in all of Erythem that has a diamond fractal is Goddess Elina. It is an honor passed on from previous rulers of the southern lands. An honor that Lassia did not look forward to inheriting. She loves her role as a healer.

"Hey everyone! I'm Lassia, your healer. You can call me Lass," Lassia introduces herself.

They all seem uninterested and continue their hushed conversations. One of the soldiers hops onto the platform. He has a square jar, shaved face, muscles for days and a little more bling on his armor than the rest. This dude must be the leader of this shit show.

"Pay attention! We are about to leave the courtyard…" his voice trails off in Lassia's ears.

I can see his dick…fuck! His grey pants are tight around his muscular legs. His impressive length is very visibly causing a perfect outline of just what this soldier has to offer. *I wonder how much bigger it gets.* She couldn't stop staring. Drool starts to pool in her lower lip as she lets her mind wander. She envisioned him towering over her as she was on her knees before him. He would make every decision. All she had to do was be a good girl for him and suck his cock. Her mind went deeper and deeper into the fantasy. *Oh my god, do I have a role-play kink? Fuck…*

"Let's meet again at first light to begin our journey," the soldier says as he hops off the platform.

Lassia recovers from her daydream and places her supplies and bag in the wagon. She goes to the kitchen to grab some dinner and heads to her room. The night is growing weary. Lass is tossing and turning in her bed. Her body is filled with excitement, anxiety, and something more. *I am so fucking wet right now. I can't stop thinking about that guy's dick. His cock is probably delicious.* Her left hand begins to caress her breasts as her right hand trails down her tight belly. She pinches her nipples and lets out a small whimper while the other hand finally reaches her warm cunt. She plunges two fingers into her pussy and curls them to apply pressure to her g spot. Her thumb is circling her aching clit. Moans and growls escape her throat as she increases speed and intensity. *God! I wish I had his cock in my mouth AND in my pussy right now.* Out of desperation for more, she took her left hand off of her breasts and sucked on her middle digit. She positions herself to be bent over her knees. Then she places that saliva coated digit in her ass. *OOOOOooooh, YES!* The added sensation of being fuller gave her the last push she needed. She came with a grunt that bordered that of an orc. Covered in sweat and cum, she cleans herself up and finally falls asleep.

Morning comes too soon. Lass is barely awake but still manages to get to the courtyard at first light. Her fellow quest-mates seem to be ready to go but for some reason no one is moving. She looks around to see who was missing. *Where is that Greek God of a man?* At last, the soldier from the night before appears on horseback. Lassia nearly chokes when she sees the man galloping towards her like a figment of her imagination.

"You are Lassia, right? The healer?" he asks with a sweet smile.

"Y..yes, that's me," she stumbles out of her mouth.

I gotta get it together. Come on, bitch!

"Great! I will have you ride in the middle of the convoy. This will keep you protected and in the best position to respond to any health issues that may arise during our journey," he explains.

"Yes sir!" she says while attempting a military salute.

Fucking kill me now.

The soldier awkwardly returns the salute, forcing a smile to ease the painful moment they just shared. He trots to the front of the crowd and gives directions on how they will be formed up for the journey. Lass' eyes stalk him like prey. She is not a virgin, by any means, but she is very particular about who beds her. Her mind loves to wonder about crazy sex with any man that looks even remotely fuckable. However, her legs only open to those that get to know her heart. The number of men that have garnered that privilege can be counted on one hand. Something is off now. Ever since the Sacred Seven entered the atmosphere, she has had an increased sex drive. Maybe her heart was no longer a requirement. All she knew was that her brain would not stop replaying the images of her sucking that soldier's cock. *I wonder what he tastes like.* Lassia's mind continues to wander as she gets into position and the convoy begins to move.

This is Lassia's first time leaving Idyll. Her skill level was reaching a point where she would no longer be able to grow within the confines of her home. Her talent will finally be put to the test, in the real world. She clutched her malachite and looked back to see the ancient canopies blending with the horizon. *This is the furthest I have ever been from home. I'm gonna miss it. Now let's suck this quest's dick.* She let out a small chuckle. The female orc miner riding next to her gave her a confused look. *She probably thinks I am crazy.* The orc opened her mouth, as if to ask a question, then shut it without saying a word. *Yup. She thinks I'm crazy.* Lassia lets out another chuckle. The orc starts to laugh. Lassia starts to laugh at the orc's laugh and now the orc is laughing even harder. These two women are laughing hysterically at absolutely nothing, and it's the best thing ever.

"Hi," the orc says while trying to contain her laughter.

"Hey there," Lassia replies while moving her head in a circular motion. Still holding in laughter.

"I am Helda. Miner extraordinaire," the orc says.

"I'm Lassia, the healer. Nice to meet you," Lassia replies.

"A healer? That's sick! Can you cure a fat ass?" the orc laughs.

"Well, that depends. Do you think an ass can be too fat?" Lass says with a cocky smile.

"Shit. I guess not," Helda says with a surprised face.

"You're welcome," Lassia says with a bow.

"Wait! For what?" Helda says with a confused look.

"I cured a fat ass by making you believe there is no such thing. So… you're welcome," Lassia laughs.

"The fuck? Hah, are you drunk?" Helda says with a hissing laughter through her teeth.

"I barely slept. I am not okay," Lassia says before forcing a tired laugh.

"Girl, you want to hop on my horse and just sleep on me?" Helda suggests.

"Are you for real right now?" Lassia asks.

"Get over here. Let mama take care of you," Helda smirks.

"Did we just become best friends?" Lassia's eyes barely open.

"Take it easy, human," Helda says before laughing.

Lassia hops over to Helda's horse and takes a much needed nap while holding on to her new friend. Helda used a rope to secure her new "backpack" in place. She made sure Lassia's horse was tied up to hers, and then she resumed her leisurely ride in the convoy. A couple hours passed before they reached the first planned stop in the route. Helda carefully woke Lassia to let her know they had reached the checkpoint. Lass stretches her arms with an arched back and a yawn. *Fuck, I needed that.*

"How did you sleep, Lassia?" Helda asks.

"Amazing! You make a great bed," Lassia replies.

"Just what every woman wants to hear," Helda smiles.

They both laugh at the exchange.

Lassia's eye catches the soldier looking at her. *Oh shit! Is he checking me out? Act cool.* She stops laughing and hops off Helda's horse. The soldier starts making his way towards the ladies.

"Hey, is that soldier guy coming?" Lass asks Helda who is still on her horse.

"The cute one? Yea, why?" Helda asks.

"Shit, I think he knows I was staring at his cock last night," Lassia whispers.

"What the fuck did you just say? I need details!" Helda exclaims.

"Not now! Act normal," Lassia hisses.

They fake a conversation and light laughter as the soldier approaches. He maneuvers himself to be in front of Lassia, who is coincidentally on her knees, fake tying her sandals. *Stay cool, relax. He didn't see you.* She looks up to find his cock less than a foot away, outlined in his tight grey pants. She does her best to not linger on it and keep looking higher up, where his face is.

"Excuse me, I just wanted to apologize for not introducing myself earlier. I am Captain Lutrix, at your service," he smiles.

"Oh, well it is nice to formally meet you Captain. I think you are great," Lassia stutters.

"I beg your pardon?" Lutrix says with a confused smile.

"Nothing. Nice to meet you," Lass says after a quick recovery.

Pull it the fuck together, bitch.

The soldier turns to Helda and pauses for a moment. He does not acknowledge her. He turns on his heel and walks away.

"Fuck that guy!" Helda mutters.

"What? Why?" a dazed Lassia asks.

"He is one of them," Helda says with a clear sadness on her expression.

"One of what? Hot as fuck?" Lass replies with her arms up in the air.

"Nay, Lass, he is a purist," Helda explains.

"I don't like the sound of that. What is a purist?" Lassia asks with a worried look on her face.

"A purist is a human that thinks that cohabitation with orcs is a mistake," Helda explains.

"That is just awful! Orcs are amazing people," Lassia says.

"That is nice of you to say, my human friend. Luckily, the few purists that remain are too afraid to be exposed. They tend to keep their opinions to themselves," Helda continues.

"Did you think I was a purist?" Lassia asks.

"No!" she let out a snort. "You are just a sweet, delusional girl."

"Hey! Fuck you, bitch!" Lassia snaps with laughter, quickly followed by Helda's. "Fuck him, then! I bet his cock tastes like shit," Lassia says while making a gagging motion.

"Probably, considering he's gay," Helda says with minimal care on her face.

"What? How do you know that? Can orcs sense gayness?" Lass asks with great confusion.

Helda let out a huge laugh and pointed at the Captain. He is at the back of the convoy making out with one of the other soldiers. Lass' jaw drops further than she thought possible. *Why am I annoyed AND turned on right now?* She took a deep breath in and then out. She turns to Helda and scoffs with laughter. Helda smiles back at her and gestures towards the horses. Lassia hops on her horse and goes right back to staring at the two gentlemen. The convoy begins to move to the next checkpoint.

chapter 4
KYSIUS

Leaving home is always a welcome escape. Kysius never truly felt at home in Ferric. He loved his father and Bron, but the only thing keeping him there was his disdain for Idyll. He had already been riding for two days on his quest for the Sacred. It is up to him to formulate the plan for when they get there. Somehow, he had not been able to effortlessly make a plan like he normally would. Something is clouding his mind. The objective is fast approaching and he needed to figure it out. *I hope we can lift this fucking thing. Shit! I forgot to bring the crane. This is going to suck massive dick.* He indeed had not been his usual sharp self since the Sacred appeared. Ky looked around at what his convoy of mercenaries looked like. *I should've brought more mercs.* The size of the gemstone is unknown. This could pose quite the issue. Luckily, it is protocol to send a second party with double the amount of men if four days passed with no contact. Kysius knew he had that safety net and that gave him peace of mind.

The sun was approaching the horizon. Kysius called for a halt to set up camp for the night. Once everyone was settled, a meeting was held to go over the plan. They all gathered around a makeshift table, a large tarp draped over a few barrels.

"Based on what I am told, we should be arriving at the crash site around noon. Let's go around the table and get a status update from everyone on their responsibilities," says Ky.

As the mercenaries took turns giving their updates, Ky found himself thinking of home. He is specifically remembering the last moment he shared with Bron. They have been friends for twenty-three years. He found himself thinking back to the day they met. Bron was in a dirty alley trying to save a baby chicken from a snake. Kysius had been walking by and heard the little seven-year-old human boy yelling at the snake while throwing rocks at it. Ky felt the urge to help the boy. As he approached Bron from behind, the boy turned around and gasped in fear. Ky quickly tried to calm Bron down and show that he was only there to help.

"Please don't hurt me! I don't want any trouble," said a scared young Bron.

"It's okay, human. I am here to help," young Kysius responded.

"Y...you are?" Bron said with a tremble.

"Watch this," Ky responded with a devilish grin.

The young orc walked up to the snake without a hitch and grabbed it by the neck. The snake wiggled frantically, trying to bite his hand to earn its freedom. Kysius looked back at Bron and smiled. Bron's face turned from fear to a hesitant smile. While keeping his smile and eyes fixated on Bron, instead of the angry serpent in his hand, Kysius made a violent jerking motion that killed the snake in one fell swoop. That simple moment sparked a trust and appreciation between the two. From that day forward, they would meet at the alleyway to get into whatever trouble they could get away with. They developed a saying, "don't get caught." That set the tone for their long friendship.

Ky often noticed moments between them that seemed more than just friendly, but he never said anything to Bron. He feared his best friend might want more than Kysius was willing to give. *I love my boy, but I don't know what his deal is.* One of the gemologists taps him on the shoulder, breaking him out of his deep thoughts. He looks up to see everyone staring at him with expectation. With a quick clearing of his throat, he addresses the group. "Alright! Sounds like we are all good to go for tomorrow. Get some rest. We leave at first light."

Ky decides to go for a walk. It is a calm night with a slight breeze. Their encampment is right next to a lake surrounded by a few scattered trees. *A stroll round the lake could help clear my head.* As he walks along the water, he catches a glimpse of his half-human, half-orc reflection. He scoffs at the sight and throws a rock at it. The ripples send waves across the lake. His eyes trail them as he contemplates his existence. *Why am I the only half-blood that has survived? Who could love me? Will I ever meet someone who makes me truly happy? I am getting tired of these meaningless hookups. They feel good for all of thirty minutes until I cum. Post nut clarity is a bitch!* His entire life, he has never known love; only women starving for his lust. As the most handsome orc, he got a lot of attention from both human and orc females. All of which he had no problem pleasuring and getting his slice of Heaven. In the end, it was never enough for him. He would end every experience at the bar talking to Bron. That was the highlight of it all, sharing the bad experiences with his best friend. The love and laughs shared between them was how Ky stayed positive. They often joked about turning gay to end the vicious cycle of women who failed to leave an impression. Kysius treated it as a joke but there was always a hint of truth. After all, Bron is one of only two people he would die for. Not to mention, Bron is a very attractive human. Ky's eyes finally fall upon the encampment that is now on the other side of the lake. He notices a commotion and starts heading towards it.

"Troll!!! GET UP, EVERYONE!!! THERE IS A TROLL!!" a mercenary screams, trying to alert everyone.

"Quick! Light some arrows. Ready your bows!" another merc ordered.

Kysius arrives at the camp and is trying to get a hold of the situation. There are people running around half dressed, with weapons at the ready. One of the gemologists is standing in front of his tent in his nightgown, holding a frying pan, looking terrified. Ky walks up to him, hoping to find out what's going on. "Espacio, what the fuck is going on? Why are you in a nightgown holding a frying pan? Did someone spike the mead again?" Ky asks in an annoyed and confused fashion.

"T..th...there i..is.. a t...troll," the elderly gemologist barely got the words out.

"Where?" Ky asked abrasively.

Espacio simply shrugs his shoulders with a frown on his face. Ky turns away from the gemologist and looks for the man that was yelling in the center of the camp. As he got closer, he could actually hear the words coming from the man's mouth.

"We need everyone ready to fight! The troll could strike at any moment!" the merc continued to shout

"You! What is this about a troll? Why are you commanding my men?" asks an angry Kysius

"I'm sorry sir, but this is an emergency and I couldn't find you," he says nervously.

"Very well. Get down from that crate and shut the fuck up. Show me this troll you speak of," Ky directs.

The mercenary hopped down and drew his sword. He motioned Ky to follow him. People were still running around like they were preparing for a full on fortress defense. Kysius figured he would let them keep their panic until he figures out if there is an active threat or not.

"Right over there, sir. I saw it run into that cave while I was taking a piss. He saw me and started walking towards me. It only ran away when Caijin showed up to take a piss of his own," Espacio explains.

"Okay, stay here, human," Ky says in a condescending way.

Orcs and trolls had a complicated relationship. Troll's were once great allies to the orcs. Then, when the humans arrived, everything changed. The trolls felt that humans were beneath them. Such small, weak creatures did not deserve their help. This was the view of most trolls during that period and it caused a rift. Orcs had an alliance with humans and that caused an issue with the trolls. That sparked a small war between humans and trolls. Orcs decided to stay out of it. With the majority of trolls living in the northern part of the continent, it fell to the humans of Ferric to eradicate them. Having all that responsibility with no help from Idyll further solidified the divide between North and South. The people of Idyll wanted no part in a war against trolls. However, they also felt no desire to align themselves with creatures that harbored so much negativity. After nearly five years of bloodshed, the trolls' numbers dwindled down to extinction levels. Due to their low numbers, they went into hiding in the midlands. The remaining trolls were rumored to kill travelers that crossed their paths, just for fun or a snack. The general rule of thumb was to kill a troll before it kills you, were you to come across one. This barbaric rule is not one that Kysius agreed with.

Ky makes his way into the cave. It is cold and dark. The cave walls are covered in shimmering red glitter. The ceiling has spires with the same red glint coming down. Hanging from the spires are clusters of bats. *You can smell the guano and hear the scattered chirping. I fucking hate caves.* He continued to press into the cave, keeping his wits about him. His senses are on high alert, looking for the troll. The sounds of tumbling rocks in the distance catch his attention. He turns his head to the left, to see what caused the movement. There is nothing there. As he turns back around, he feels a hot breath on his right shoulder. *The troll is right next to me and he is breathing on me, isn't he? Fuck me sideways.* Kysius steadies himself and grabs hold of his tourmaline. Then, in a calm and confident voice, he speaks to the troll. "Hey buddy, I'm just here to talk." He keeps his hand on his stone at the ready.

"I'm not your buddy, guy. What the fuck do you want?" asks the almost eight foot, six hundred pounds of pure muscle, troll.

"Well, first of all, I am not your buddy, pal. Since you want to be so specific. You scared the shit out of my mercenaries and now they think you are going to eat them all," says an appalled Kysius, with a loosening grip on his stone.

"Listen here, pal, I was minding my own business when a dickhead human started taking a piss on my favorite tree,"the troll says, clearly annoyed.

"I am sorry he went pee pee on the wrong tree, okay? Now, do I need to worry about you coming over and eating or raping my guys while we sleep?" Ky asks.

"No promises, pal. You know how much trolls love to rape and eat humans," the troll says with a sinister chuckle.

"Hah! I like you, bro. What's your name?" Ky asks through his laughter.

"Don't call me bro, dude. My name is Botistanuckashuk," the troll demands.

"Damn, bro! Sorry, I mean dude. That name is fucking cray!" Ky laughs.

"It was my grandfather's name. I take great pride in my name, but most people call me Botuk," Botistanuckashuk says.

"No, let me try it. Botiskanik...." Ky struggles to get the name correctly. "Fuck that! Botuk it is," says a defeated Kysius.

They both engulfed in laughter at their exchange. Botuk offered him some food and refreshment. Kysius explains why he was there with his group of mercs. After some light conversation and full bellies, Kysius has convinced the troll to come to the camp to help ease the rest of the group. As they approached the camp, Ky had to order everyone to stand down. One merc accidentally let an arrow fly and it hit Botuk on his left forearm. It barely penetrated his tough exterior. Botuk removed the arrow and chuckled.

"Do you want this back? Or should I keep it as a token of our time together?" he smirked. The troll toyed with the mercenary that is seconds away from pissing himself in fear.

"No one move a fucking muscle! He comes in peace. The next person to attack him will have to answer to my tourmaline!" Kysius says with fire in his eyes.

Every single person present stood as still as statues at the mention of his tourmaline. The amount of pain and agony that is rumored to be emitted from that stone is worse than torture. It was definitely a large part of why Kysius is so powerful, respected and feared. Kysius motioned to his men to lower their guard. They oblige. He then waved the troll forward, to go deeper into the encampment. As they approach the center, Kysius hops on the same crate that the merc was yelling from earlier. Quiet chatter broke out amongst the mercs

"Listen up! This is Botuk. He is not going to eat or rape you. Don't make him change his mind. Savvy?" Ky explains. A sea of silence took hold of the crowd. "Yes? No? Do…you…understand?"

Uncoordinated ayes start pouring from the gaggle. The response made Kysius smile as he hopped down from the crate. He then gestured to Botuk. They headed over to Ky's tent. "What would it take for you to join us?" Kysius asks as he hands the troll a mug of mead.

"Join you? Aren't you worried about me eating and raping people who piss me off?" Botuk responds.

"I definitely don't want you eating my men," Ky lets out a chuckle.

Botuk laughed at the insinuation.

"What about after we complete your quest? Am I to just walk back home alone with nothing to show for my efforts?" Botuk inquires.

"Hell no! You can stay with me, in Ferric," Ky answers.

"Are you drunk, orc? I wouldn't last a day in Ferric," Botuk says with a confused expression.

"You would be under my protection. It will be fine!" Ky says while giving a cocky smirk.

"And who are you to hold that much power?" Botuk inquires.

Kysius shows the troll his tourmaline. Botuk almost falls back, trying to gain distance from the evil gemstone. "How can you hold that?! That thing is pure evil!" Botuk had a hint of fear on his face.

Trolls had a fear of gemstones ever since the humans used them during their war. Harnessing the power of gemstones is only possible through jewel crafting, which is only done by humans. That made it impossible for trolls to ever use the stones to their advantage. All gems symbolized for trolls were pain and defeat.

"Calm down, Bo. Can I call you Bo? I am a half-blood. I have trained my whole life to harness and control my tourmaline," Ky says with confidence

"Gods help you. You have some fucking demons, Kysius. And no, don't call me Bo. I am no weak bitch," Botuk snaps at Kysius

"Fair enough. So, will you join me or what?" Ky asks with an eager look.

"Fuck it. I'm sick of that damn cave anyway. Those bats are loud as fuck!" says Botuk.

"And they stink!" Ky added.

FRACTAL

The duo laughed and finished their drinks. They went to their respective beds and got some much needed rest.

FRACTAL

chapter 5

HELDA

The convoy is moving along on schedule. Just two more days until it arrives at its destination. Lassia and Helda have become attached at the hip. The ladies have created quite the bond during the journey. They even started playing a game to pass the time called "Moan Whore Moan." The point of the game is to see who can moan louder than the other without causing a reaction from the surrounding quest-mates. So far, the score was three to two in favor of Helda. Lassia was a bit too enthusiastic when taking her turns. She enjoyed forcing Helda into using an uncomfortable volume. It became harder and harder to get a reaction from people as they caught on to the game. This made the game even more fun for the girls. The moans would reach ungodly volume before getting a reaction. Game six is about to start. Lass looks at Helda and gives her a menacing look.

"What the fuck are you up to?" Helda asks with uncertainty in her eyes.

"Let's up the ante. First person to moan loud enough to get Captain Lutrix's attention wins," says Lass with a bewildered look.

"You crazy bitch. I'm in! Ladies first," Helda says with determination

"Hah, pussy!" Lassia laughs.

Lutrix was about one hundred yards away. A decent distance to cover with a human voice, not to mention the wind blowing in the opposite direction of him. *There is no way this bitch can reach him with that cute little throat of hers.* Nothing can deter Lassia from proving a point. She let out a loud and sexually charged moan that surely would reach his ears. To her surprise, no reaction from the Captain. Just a few members of the convoy rolling their eyes and others laughing.

"No shot! That was all I had. I'm even wet right now," Lassia bites her lip and giggled.

"Let a real woman give it a shot," Helda smirks. Helda took a couple deep breaths and let out a bellowing moan. It was so intense that the vibrations could be felt in your bones. At the front of the formation, Captain Lutrix quickly turned his head in search of the source. Helda exploded in laughter as they locked eyes. The gaze lingers for a moment. Lutrix's eyes did not emit hate. They gave a sense of yearning. Helda immediately broke eye contact. *What the fuck was that? Why did it look like he wanted me? In no world would a purist ever touch me!* Lassia crossed her arms with a fake exaggerated pout on her face.

"Fine, you win. I didn't know you could make such a noise, girl," says the beautiful Princess.

"I can do a lot of things with this throat," Helda says with a wink.

"You dirty slut!" says a laughing Lass.

Helda places her hand on her heart and gasps, as to imply she is offended. "How rude!" Helda says as she breaks into laughter with her new bestie.

The convoy suddenly halts. People start dismounting and take their last break before making their last push for the day. Lassia overhears some of the soldiers talking about the Captain being from Muria. She had heard stories about the far away land, full of magic and opportunity. It was rare to meet someone who would leave such a place for more than just a short period. *I need to find out what that look was about earlier.* He was surrounded by soldiers and this stop was not meant to be a long one. She decided to wait until they camped for the night to confront him alone.

The convoy is now approaching its final checkpoint of the day. Helda had spent the last couple of miles in contemplative silence.

"What's on your mind, babe? You okay? Haven't really said much since the last checkpoint," Lass cautiously asks her friend.

"I'm sorry. Just deep in thought," Helda responds.

"Care to share? Judgment free zone here," Lassia says with her hand on her heart.

"Remember when I kicked your ass in Moan Whore Moan?" Helda asks.

"Vaguely," Lass responds.

"When the Captain looked at me, I think he gave me 'fuck-me eyes,'" Helda winces,

"Excuse the fuck out of me?" says a wide eyed Lassia.

"I know, right? I must have been seeing things," Helda bites her lip.

"How did it make you feel?" Lass asks.

"Umm, I was kind of into it," Helda says. She looks away while answering.

"You little whore!" Lassia sneers.

"What? You imagined sucking his dick first. I don't want to hear it!" Helda snaps playfully.

"True, true. I guess you should just go fuck him now," she says lazily.

"Stop!" Helda laughs.

I definitely want to though.

They finally arrived at their final stop for the night. Lassia was very eagerly looking around for something. *What is this girl doing?* She kept looking around desperately through her belongings.

"Got it!" Lassia yells.

"Got what?" Helda asks.

"I brought some of my perfume, just in case," Lassia says while giving a cute shrug. Shes walks over to Helda and sprays her with it. *Oh my god this is fucking strong.* Helda sneezed and coughed a bit. *Oh, it's not that bad actually.* Lassia laughed as she witnessed her friend have a roller coaster of emotions in reaction to the perfume.

"Now we just need to fix your hair," Lassia continues.

"My hair is fine, Lassia," Helda says with a dismissive look.

"Uh, excuse me. It sure as fuck isn't! Get over here. Let's give that hunk of a man something to grab on to. Ooooh, a French braid will do!" Lassia orders.

"A French what?" a very confused Helda responds.

"Bitch, just stay still and let mama take care of you, okay?"Lassia laughs.

"Fine," says a defeated Helda.

Over the next thirty minutes, Lassia gives Helda an entirely new look. It was now time for Helda to see the new her. *Wow, I look…pretty.* Helda was not an ugly orc, by any means. But she never had someone take the time to beautify her as a lady. She spent most of her life working the mines with her father. Her physique was amazing. She was curvy in all the right places and had a tight core. Her face, on the other hand, was just the average orc face. With Lassia's help, now she was able to see all her best facial features shine. *I don't know what to say to her. Thanks is nowhere near enough. I have never seen myself like this. Cared for like this.* Helda looks back at a smiling Lassia, who was glowing with pride, and starts crying.

"Oh no! What happened, babes? Do you not like it?" asks a worried

Lass.

Helda tries to compose herself as she sniffles and carefully wipes the streams running down her face. "I have never had anyone do this for me before," Helda says through tears.

"I'm so sorry, hun. Everyone deserves to be cared for and made to feel beautiful," says a heartbroken Lass.

"My mother died when she gave birth to me. I have never had a female figure in my life. All my friends were males. I never fit in with women. You are pretty much my first real female friend," says Helda as she composed herself.

"Well, that is their loss. Fuck those bitches! You are amazing and I can't wait for you to show them just how amazing by fucking that Captain," Lassia says with encouragement.

Helda chuckled and took a deep breath. She stood up straight and exhaled. Lassia came over and did some final readjustments to get her back to pristine condition. *Okay, lets fuck this pig!* Helda made her way towards the Captain's tent. As she approaches, she notices he is not there. She pauses for a second and looks around. She hears a grunt from the trees behind the tent. She maneuvers to see what made the noise. *Oh dear! Captain Lutrix is getting his dick sucked by one of his soldiers.* He is completely naked, leaning on a tree. The moonlight is hitting his body perfectly to accentuate all his muscles and veins. They are pulsing as he strains with pleasure from the mouth that is wrapped around his cock. *Should I leave or stay?* Helda hesitates for a second but then realizes she has a small pool between her legs. *Fuck this is actually really hot.* The soldier is slowing his pace and the Captain is seemingly getting annoyed.

"Don't slow down. Suck harder, faster," the Captain demands.

"I'm sorry, sir. I don't know what I am doing. Please don't fire me." pleaded the soldier, maybe nineteen years of age.

"Just go! Do not speak a word of this, or I will have more than just your job," Lutrix says in anger.

He began pulling his pants back up with a disappointed look on his face. *Fuck it!* Helda lunges towards him and pushes him against the tree. His cock still hard and poking at her right thigh. She was about a foot taller than him.

"Are you a purist?" she demanded.

"What? No!" Lutrix responds.

"Don't lie to me, Captain. I can smell lies on humans!" Helda feigns with conviction.

"I swear to you! My best friend is an orc," he pleads.

"Then why did you treat me like I didn't exist when you went to meet Lassia?" she inquires with a snarl in her voice.

"Be…Because….Ah, fuck it to hell. I thought you were so fucking hot and I had to walk away to not flirt with you openly. If word got out that I was attracted to orcs, I would never be able to face my parents," he answered frantically.

He thinks I am hot? Holy shit. Helda places a hand on his throat and applies a small amount of pressure. She feels Lutrix's cock stiffen. *He likes this, huh?* She takes her other hand and grabs hold of his impressive length and begins to slowly stroke it. The Captain lets out a growling moan.

"So why do you keep kissing and fucking your soldiers? Are you gay? Bi? Bored?" she asks.

"B..Bo..Bored. Fuck, you are so good at that," he says as he looked down to watch her stroke him.

"I have more questions, but right now I just need your cock in my mouth,"Helda says. She gets on her knees. She realizes his cock is still too low for her to put in her mouth. She lifts him up and places his legs over shoulders. Captain Lutrix is now straddling Helda's face and he lets out a small yelp at the surprise. Helda is taking every delicious inch he has to offer. Her tongue swirling around the tip of his cock for a moment, before slurping him all the way to the back of her throat. *God, he is so big and juicy.*

"This is too good. Fuck!" Captain squirms.

Helda pulled her head back, letting his cock fling upward. It was covered in saliva and pulsing.

"You better not cum until I tell you to!" Helda commands.

"Yes, ma'am," he replies.

"Good boy," Helda smiles.

She swallows him again in desperation for more of his length. It's so velvety and hard. Indulging every second, she decided it was time for him to take a turn. She lifts him off her shoulders and lays him on the ground. Helda removes all her clothes, exposing herself for him to admire her gorgeous body.

"You are the most beautiful woman I have ever seen," Lutrix says in awe.

Helda blushed but quickly regained her composure and lowered herself onto his face. "That's nice. Now prove it!" Helda says as she lowered her wet, throbbing pussy onto his precious human lips.

He hungrily accepts her offering by lapping his tongue all over her opening. His lips caressing hers as the tip of his tongue plays with her clit. Helda moans in appreciation. *This guy knows what he is doing.* He sneakily slid two fingers inside of her aching pussy. Helda gasped. She welcomed the surprise digits and started to grind her hips on his face, elevating the experience. Lutrix noticed her enthusiasm and decided to up the ante. He licked a third finger and slowly pressed it into her ass. *What the fuck?! No!* Helda reached down and slapped the unwelcomed digit out of her ass.

"That is not for fingers. Bad boy," Helda says between quick breaths.

"Yes, ma'am. Sorry, ma'am," he responds.

Helda lifted herself off of his face. The Captain panicked and sat up, thinking his anal play backfired. She looked back at him and pushed him back down. Turning away from him, she gave his cock a few more licks and then spit on it. Lutrix was moaning uncontrollably. She then positioned herself above his cock and sat on it.

"Holy shit! You are so tight!" Captain says in disbelief.

He looked down to watch the show. To his surprise, it was not her pussy he was feeling. *Mmmm this cock feels so good in my ass.* Helda loves feeling a thick cock in her ass, not little fingers that only tickled. She moved up and down in slow and smooth fashion.

"You like that asshole?" she asks with a devilish smile.

"Oh my god, yes!" he responds, out of breath.

The motion transitioned from vertical to a horizontal grinding motion. This was Helda's favorite way to take a cock in the ass. She could feel he was getting close. Her legs started shaking. His cock throbbing harder and harder. His balls were tucked into his abdomen. She reached down and pulled them out and fondled them. It was enough to send her over the edge. She released her sweet cum all over his hardened cock with a bellowing moan.

"FUCK!!!" she growls.

"Now cum in my ass, like a good boy," she demands.

His balls went back into his abdomen and his cock pulsed three more times as she rode him out. *I feel something warm in my ass. God it's so good.* Captain Lutrix had released his full load in her ass. Helda carefully stood up and laid beside him on the forest floor.

"That was amazing," Captain says after a deep breath in and out.

"You were not too bad yourself," she replies with a joyful giggle.

They laid together for a second, enjoying the moment they just shared in comfortable silence. *I can't wait to tell Lassia.* Helda got up and got dressed. Lutrix scrambled to meet her pace and get dressed.

"My name is Myka, by the way," the Captain says.

"Helda," she responds.

"Do you want to do this again or...?" he asks with a nervous laugh.

"We will see. I am no one's secret,"Helda replies.

She walked away with her head up high and an ass full of cum.

FRACTAL

chapter 6
KYSIUS

The sun has been especially hot today. Kysius and company have just arrived at the estimated crash site, with no Sacred Seven in sight. Ky orders everyone to walk one hundred yards in each direction, then signal back with crossed arms for "no" or a thumbs up for "yes." He waits impatiently for the mercs to reach their respective spots. Botuk is standing next to him, scanning the horizon for anything shiny.

"Do you see anything?" Kysius asks his new troll friend.

"Nope."

"Fuck! I knew this was just an estimate but I really hoped it was accurate," Ky complains.

"Be patient my friend. We will find your rock," Botuk responds.

All the mercenaries had reached their marks and all held up crossed arms.

"Mother fucker!" Ky yells in disappointment.

He ordered the entire party to move another mile south. Everyone regrouped and started their movement. As they passed the half mile point, Kysius started feeling strange. *Fuck, my head hurts like a bitch. Why do I feel nauseous, all of a sudden?* Then he realized what it was. He was close. He halted the convoy and told everyone to do another one hundred yard search. As all the mercs began their walk, one of them stopped about thirty yards away.

"I got something!" he yells with his right hand in the air, forming a thumbs up.

"Let's go!" Ky cheered.

Everyone collapsed onto the position. The merc points towards the object he spotted. At the end of his fingertip was a massive crystalline rock that had every color swirled together. The most predominant color was a light purple, almost dark pink. Some areas were yellow, some black. It was the most precious gemstone for a reason. It was hard to say it was one specific color. The shape reassembled a jagged icicle.

Overjoyed with the sight, they all stormed to it. Kysius was trying to get over his illness, likely caused by the energy the Sacred Seven has. He takes a strong swig of his mead and pushes through to join everyone at the stone. They are all in awe of the mythical gemstone before their eyes. Kysius immediately orders everyone to not touch it. He tells some mercenaries to do a perimeter search to make sure they don't encounter any surprises. Another group of men are told to set up the camp and start devising a plan to pull the rock out of the ground and haul it back home. Ky is worried he does not have the manpower and tools for the job, but is open to any ideas.

"You think you can lift that thing, bud?" he asks.

"I can try, but you said not to touch it," Botuk says with his arms crossed.

"Are you trolling me? I don't like getting trolled," Kysius says sarcastically.

"I'll go try," Botuk replies while laughing to his friends punny joke.

Botuk approaches the Sacred. He heaves and pulls with all his might but could not force even the smallest nudge. This gemstone was extremely heavy. It would take more than a swole troll to take it out of the ground.

"That needs dug out, brother. No creature on this earth can muscle that out of the ground," Botuk says.

"We don't even know how far that goes into the ground. It might be too heavy to lift with our numbers and tools," says a worried Ky.

Botuk shrugged at his friend's comment. Kysius goes to help set up camp and rethink his strategy. He knows he has a few days to figure something out and send word to his father. If he didn't succeed in getting the Sacred out and ready for transport, he would just need to wait for the reinforcements to arrive. Unfortunately, that would take too long. Kysius had just dispatched the messenger to let his father know they made it to the Sacred. That meant he had to wait four days to activate the reinforcement protocol, plus three more days for them to reach the crash site. *Ugh an entire fucking week, if I can't figure this shit out. Plus four more days to travel home. I could use some pussy right about now.* He told everyone that was able bodied to start digging. Once he had the team that came back from checking the perimeter, he had them go forage for food and supplies.

During their journey, they got raided by wolves. They took most of their fresh meat and two mercenaries lost their lives during the skirmish. It was Botuk that saved the day. He grabbed a nearby branch that resembled a club and swatted the wolves away. His swing was so powerful, he managed to kill one of them and that caused the rest to flee. That earned him the respect of all the mercenaries in the party. He hasn't been able to wipe the smile off his face since. Botuk was so proud of that moment that he kept the branch as a weapon and keepsake.

Kysius wants to make sure they are prepared for the seven day wait, if necessary. He calls a meeting with the more experienced members of the party.

"We need to plan for a seven day stay out here. I am open to suggestions on how to make this easy for everyone and avoid some bullshit breaking out while we are here. I don't need in-fighting nor people dying of thirst, hunger, or cold," Kysius opens up with.

"That's going to be tough. Most people here expected a seven day quest, not twice that!" the most seasoned merc replies.

"Luckily, we are near a river for water and these lands have plenty of animals to hunt. The only issue I see is we don't have many hunting weapons. We need to fashion some," says another merc.

"Aye, we need to fashion hunting weapons and make sure we keep people's tempers in check," Kysius responds.

"Regarding the cold, we can have people double up in their tents. Nothing beats body heat," adds the other merc in the room.

"You can say that again," Botuk butts in with a wink.

I fucking love this guy.

"Alright, alright, alright. Seems like we have all our bases covered. Let's get to work, people," Kysius says with confidence.

With all the new orders sent out, all progress on the dig was halted until they had the necessary supplies to survive. Priority one is hunting weapons and food. Then firewood. Then we can worry about digging and keeping everyone in check. The plan was solid. So long as all the mercs didn't get impatient and kill each other, all was well.

The first night went by without a hitch. No real progress was done on the dig, but hunting weapons were fashioned and the men seemed to be in high spirits. Kysius no longer felt any illness. Maybe it wasn't the gemstone. *Wait, am I pregnant? Haha stupid!* It was time to put the weapons to use and go on the first hunt. Considering their numbers were already small, they all went together to this hunting party. The only problem with hunting in a large group is how loud it can be. Animals in the midlands were very skittish and had phenomenal hearing. These men were used to hunting in Ferric, which was significantly easier. Kysius was walking towards the rear of the hunting party, alongside Botuk. They were chatting quietly about who could cum more, orcs or trolls. Up front, the mercenaries were not being very quiet. Anytime an animal was within range, someone would sneeze or cough or breathe too loud. It was a nightmare for a hunter. Eventually, the more passionate hunters started to lose their patience and started shit talking the other mercenaries. That did not take long. Ky makes his way to the front where the argument was being had.

"Okay, girls. Let's stop all this fighting. We are all pretty and going to prom," Kysius says in a sarcastic manner.

"These assholes are costing us every single chance at food," says an angry hunter.

"Alright, how about we play a game of Simon Says?" Ky asks.

"What the fuck is that?" asks one of the mercenaries.

"It means I tell you to shut the fuck up and hang out near the back of the group or you will be stuck eating scraps," Kysius says with a crazy smile.

"Okay, okay. We will move to the back and be quiet," the merc responds.

"Good girl," Ky says jokingly.

I miss saying that. I really need to get laid.

With the new shuffle of men, the hunting party continued its quest to find food. The hunters up front and the less skilled mercenaries in the back, keeping as quiet as possible. It did not take long for the hunters to land a couple of deer. *Eureka!* The men now had food for a day or two. They headed back to the camp and got to work on the deer and gemstone. The men were exhausted. Kysius even felt the need to rest. He called all the mercenaries in and ordered a three hour mandatory break. The men welcomed the opportunity to recharge. Ky did his best to keep morale high without sacrificing progress. He already knew they were not going to make the four day deadline. Sending a messenger to say just that would be a waste. Everything was going according to plan. Plan B, that is. Kysius sees Espacio walking by in his nightgown, heading to take a nap presumably.

"Espacio! No frying pan?" Ky joked.

"No sir. Not today," the elderly man chuckled and headed into his tent.

chapter 7
LASSIA

After getting all the hot gossip from Helda, Lassia was feeling a bit jealous. *My girl got some good dick last night. I love that for her. Wish I had some.* The girls were packing up their camp to make the final push to the crash site. They should be arriving by early afternoon. Everyone was excited to finally put their eyes on the fabled Sacred Seven; most of all, Lassia. The convoy started its trek to, what hopefully, was their final destination. The quest had gone off without a hitch so far. Lassia would catch Helda looking up at Lutrix on occasion. *This bitch is falling in love.* She would make kissy faces at her in a mocking way. Helda would give her the middle finger, to which Lass would respond with a tongue between her fingers. The girls would catch the Captain looking back and they would wave and giggle. It made the journey that much more enjoyable. Something about torturing a man that was clearly smitten was just fun to them.

"Are you going to hit that again?" Lassia asks

"I don't know yet. Not sure how I feel about the whole sneaking around thing," Helda says with a frown.

"That's the hottest part of it all. You get to be as slutty as you want and not have to answer to anyone about it. I would take that opportunity without hesitation!" Lass says.

"Hmm, maybe I will do it one more time," Helda says with a grin.

"Yas, bitch! That's my girl!" Lass yelled.

People around them gave them a strange look. Lass responds to them with taunting body language. *What, bitch?* Making them go back to minding their own business. *That's what I thought!* Helda just sat back on her horse and laughed at how unhinged her friend was.

"How are you a princess, dude?" Helda asks.

"What? You think royalty can't be cool and tough? Guess again, bitch. I am setting a new standard," Lassia says with a sarcastic snobby look.

"My apologies, milady," Helda says in a posh accent.

Laughter breaks out between them. The long ride to the Sacred is coming to a close. *Time flies when you are having fun. What would I do without Helda? Can I keep her?* The convoy receives a sudden halt. Everyone is trying to see what the holdup is. The girls notice the soldiers are changing their formation, no longer in two single file lines. This doesn't look good. Captain Lutrix motions for everyone to meet in the middle of the convoy.

"Listen up, everyone. We spotted an encampment next to the Sacred Seven. We are going to find out who they are and take the appropriate actions," he informs the group.

"What can we do to help?" Lassia asks.

"You can stay out of sight and wait for my men to give you the all clear," the Captain responds.

They all ran to cover, except for Lassia. *Fuck hiding. I am trained in combat and I am a healer. They need me.* She slowly worked her way up to where the soldiers were and stayed hidden from the Captain. A few of the soldiers went off to get a better look, while the rest were preparing for the worst. A few minutes passed by and the scouts came back.

"They are Ferric, sir," the scout says.

"It is as I feared. They beat us to it. What are their numbers looking like?" Lutrix asks.

"I counted eight, maybe twelve at the most," the scout responds.

"Well that is music to my ears," the captain says in relief.

The soldiers circled around the Captain as they devised the plan of attack. Lassia decided to sneak past and get closer to the enemy camp. She wanted to be nearby when the action started. By the time she got to a comfortable spot, the soldiers were running towards the camp with weapons drawn. Lass heard a man yell, "We got company!"

She saw about six men completely abandon the camp and run away in fear. *Well, that makes our lives easier. Only a few more to deal with.* Botuk stands up from under the tree he was resting in. *What the fuck! Is that a fucking troll?!* He grabs his club and starts making his way towards the soldiers but is stopped by Kysius. Lassia was too far to hear what was said but she saw the troll turn around and run like the other mercenaries. *What is going on here?* Kysius yells to the rest of his men to retreat. *Who is this guy?* He moves over to the Sacred Seven and stands with his arms crossed, unarmed. The soldiers reach the stone and surround him.

"Get on your knees, orc!" Lutrix demanded.

"I only get on my knees to eat pussy. Are you going to let me eat you, cunt?" Ky responds with a hungry look on his face.

"Detain him!" the Captain ordered.

Kysius is chained and tied to a nearby tree. Lassia comes out of hiding and finds herself face to face with Captain Lutrix. *Fuck.*

"What are you doing here? I told you to hide," Lutrix says.

"I was hiding. Just a lot closer than the rest," she slyly replies.

Lutrix scoffed. Kysius overheard and chuckled at her boldness. *What is he laughing at?* Lass makes her way over to the orc prisoner and eyes him from head to toe. *Hmmm, he looks fun.* He kept jerking his body to try to get loose but all it did was flex his muscles and make his veins pump full of blood. *He is quite handsome, for an orc. Something is different about him.*

"Hey, buddy. Are you a hybrid or something? You are too pretty to be a pure orc," Lassia asks.

"Go fuck yourself!" Ky snaps at her.

"What I do on my own time is my business, mister!" Lassia replies sarcastically.

"You have a mouth on you, don't you?" Ky asks.

"You have no idea," Lass replies with a wink.

She walked closer to Kysius and let her fingers trail the muscles on his bound arms. *He is so strong. I bet he could make me remember him for days after the deed.* Kysius jerked trying to get her hands off of him.

"How about you show me?" Ky asks with a cocky grin.

"Excuse me! I am a lady. How dare you?!" This is another sarcastic line from Lassia.

"Who are you?" Ky asks.

"I am Lassia, healer and Princess of Idyll," Lass says with pride.

"A princess, huh? That makes sense," Ky says under his breath.

"What is that supposed to mean?" Lass asks.

"Look in the mirror. You look the part," Ky sneers.

"Is that a compliment?" she asks.

"If you want it to be," he shrugs.

I don't know what to do with this guy.

"What is your name, tough guy?" Lass asks

"I am Kysius," he responds.

"Anything special about you? Or is it just Kysius?" Lass asks.

"Just Kysius," he replies.

This dude is hiding something. He is acting sus.

"Okay, just Kysius. What brings you to the Sacred Seven?" Lass demands.

"I was part of a band of mercenaries sent here by the great King Thrasus," Ky explains.

"Pssh, 'Great King' my ass," Lass says in snide.

"Hey! Watch it. That's my King you are talking about," Ky snaps.

"Touchy. Why did you tell everyone to run, including a troll? Like where the fuck did you get a troll?" Lass asks with a look of confusion.

"I didn't feel like seeing any bloodshed and the troll is just a friend. I make lots of friends," Ky replies calmly.

"I bet you do," Lass smirks. She stood there in silence for a while, trying to formulate any more questions. Eyeing him closely, looking for any clues. His clothes don't look fancy. He doesn't have weapons. *He has really strong legs. I wonder what his cock looks like. Focus, bitch! Focus!*

"Let's try this again. Are you an orc or what?" Lass pressed the issue.

"I am a hybrid. The only living one," Ky replies with an exhausted air about his words.

"Umm, I hate to break it to you, friend. You are not the only hybrid alive," Lass laughs.

"What?!" Ky looks at her with great confusion.

"Yeah, there are plenty of hybrids in Idyll. They are normally more human than orc, but hybrids nonetheless," Lass explains.

"How? I was told my whole life I was the only one," he says confused.

"Do you not have healers in Ferric?" she inquires.

"Not many. The ones we do have are drunks and only deal with battle wounds," he answered with an annoyed tone.

"There is your answer. A good healer can save a hybrid born," Lass emphasized.

The look on Kysius' face was that of a broken man. His entire life he had believed that he was the only one of his kind. He felt cheated, lied to, and disregarded. His heart filled with anger. Lassia noticed his demeanor changing. She quickly clutched her malachite and placed her other hand on his chest.

"What are you doing?" he asks through his teeth.

"Healing you," she responds.

His anger was dissipating rapidly. His heart rate and breathing slowed. She had removed all the anger and hatred that was building inside of him.

"Why did you do that?" he asks.

"Because you don't deserve to feel all that anger for something that is not your fault," she replies.

"T..Thank you. You didn't have to," Ky says.

Kysius' head fell to the ground. Feeling relief and exhaustion all at once. *Shit, did I overdo it?*

"Hey, are you still with me?" Lass asks with a worried tone.

"Yes, I just never felt this much weight off my shoulders before," Ky replies.

Lassia smiled with relief that she didn't accidentally drain some of his soul. With the information she had, she felt he wasn't a threat to her. "I am going to untie you. If you try anything, I will use this stone to give you so much stress and anxiety that you will faint and quite possibly die," she warned.

"I promise to keep my hands and feet inside the ride at all times. Unless you tell me not to," Ky says with a wink.

She looked into his human eyes and handsome features that made him look more human than some people she knew. There was a warmth in his gaze. It made her heart skip a beat. *I can't tell if I want to fuck him or marry him. I ain't mad at either.* She proceeded to remove his restraints. He rubbed his wrists, bringing circulation back to them. She glamoured at sight, when he stood up straight in front of her. *He is so tall, handsome, and muscular. Lord help me.* She did her best to hide her lady boner. She offered him some water, to which he smiled and accepted. As he drank, she watched his Adam's apple bob up and down with every swallow. She bit her lip with lust in her eyes. He caught her looking at him and he winked as he finished his drink. *Cocky little shit.*

"So, what does your mother want with the Sacred?" Kysius asks.

"STEP mother. I don't know exactly. I just wanted to be on this quest for the experience," she replies.

"Interesting. She doesn't share her plans with you?" Ky inquires.

"Sometimes," she answers.

He seemed confused that her dynamic with her stepmother wasn't the same as his with his father. Kysius gathers all the rope and chains used to tie him and neatly folds them. He carries them over to the nearest soldier that looked at him in surprise. "Here you go, buddy. I think your Daddy forgot these," he says with a smile.

"T..Thank y..you.," the soldier says after a huge gulp.

Kysius walked back over to the Princess and reached his hand out. She took it with a raised brow. *What is this guy doing? Why am I just going along with it?* He brought her to his tent. He sat on his bed and patted beside him, motioning her to take a seat next to him.

"Sit," he commanded, and she obliged.

"Take off your shirt," Ky requested.

"What? No!" she replies, covering her breasts.

Kysius stood and positioned himself in front of her. Placing a hand on her shoulder, so she could not stand up, he repeated himself with more intention.

"Take….Off…Your…Shirt…" he demanded.

Lassia started undoing her top. *What the fuck am I doing? How is he doing this to me? Why can't I stop myself?* She removed her top, baring her perfectly perky breasts for him to see.

"Good. Very good," he growled. He placed his hands on her breasts and started caressing her nipples. "You have the most beautiful nipples, Princess."

Fuck this feels good. Ugh, I love how he calls me princess.

"T..Thank you…" she replies blissfully.

He reached his left hand up to her neck. Her skin erupted in goosebumps as his hand grasped her neck with light pressure. *Oh my god, yes, yes, a million times yes.* After a moment, he placed his hand on her face and caressed her cheek with his thumb. Then he slid his hand behind her head, running his fingers through her hair. She let out a low moan and he caressed her scalp. Grabbing a handful of her hair, he tugged it back, forcing her face upward and making her yelp in pleasure. His mouth crashed against hers. Their tongues commenced a beautiful dance in their mouths. It was as if their mouths knew each other for years; a perfect ballet being performed by their lips and tongues. Lassia's mind was blank with pleasure and ecstasy. His right hand is still caressing her breasts and his left hand is holding her hair firmly to the rear. They are in their own fragment of the universe, lost in each other. Kysius senses footsteps and slowly retreats his lips, tongue, and hands. He grabs her top and carefully places it back in place. Lassia is still in a daze with her eyes closed. Helda comes around the corner and her eyes fall to Lassia still dazed.

"There you are! I have been looking for you all over the place. Who is this gentleman?" Helda asks her kiss drunk friend.

"This is K..Kysius? I'm sorry, I just need a moment," Lass replies with a blissful smile.

"I am Kysius. Your friend is pretty amazing," Kysius interjected.

"She is, is she? I am sure she will tell me all about it," Helda says with a raised brow.

Helda helps Lass gather herself and begins to walk her out of Kysius' tent. As they are walking away, Lassia turns to get another look at Ky. He waves at her and she drunkenly waves back.

Captain Lutrix storms towards Lassia. *Oh shit, this fucking guy.*

"Hi, Helda," he says with a goofy smile.

Helda waves and gives him a shy grin.

"Lassia, what in the ever loving fuck are you doing? You can't just release a prisoner of mine!" Lutrix says in an offended tone.

"Actually, I can. Don't worry, I interrogated him. He is harmless. We could use him. He is a mercenary" Lass argues.

Lutrix scoffed and opened his mouth to say more, but decided against it. He turned heel and stormed away in a huff.

FRACTAL

CHAPTER 8
KYSIUS

Shit! Fuck! Mother Fuck! Rubber Duck! Okay, think, think, think. Everyone ran to our fallback point. As long as I keep them here long enough, reinforcements will arrive and we will take the Sacred. This could work! I play nice and sabotage as needed to delay them. Yes! Perfect! Use the Idyll to do the work and we reap all the benefits. I love it when a plan comes together.

With his entire party and quest bestie, Botuk, hidden away, he could focus on plan C and stall the Idyll for four days, at the most. The mercenaries only managed to dig about forty percent of the expected depth to free the gemstone in three days. If the Idyll work at the same rate, Ferric soldiers would arrive before the Sacred is fully free. That was Kysius' hope. If all else fails, sabotage. His men were instructed to not return to the gemstone until the reinforcements arrived. Kysius knew there was a chance Idyll might have seen the flaming ball of fire fall from the sky and sent a party. He devised this brilliant plan while getting drunk with Botuk on the second night of being at the crash site. *Drunk or not, I make great plans.* This plan, while very flawed, was actually a best case scenario for Kysius. He could use this as the excuse for not getting the job done in the original timeframe. All that was left to do was focus on the task at hand. That task being Lassia and the rest of her party.

Kysius is still reeling from the moment he shared with Lassia in his tent just a few hours ago. He did not expect it to feel the way it did. Normally he doesn't feel anything when he kisses a woman. It's usually just a way to get him hard. Never had he felt something in his heart or soul. *Something is different about that girl. I need to find out what.* He went for a walk around the camp. Doing his best to not look suspicious, he lapped the gemstone, taking note of any changes the Idyllians made. Hmm, nothing crazy. It should take them more than four days with what they have here. He walks away from the stone and heads to the river. As he approaches, he hears female giggles. He quickly finds a spot closer to the source and hides himself. Lassia and Helda are in the river, nude, splashing each other playfully. *Holy shit! What a show! Two gorgeous women. A human and an orc. The perfect duo.* Kysius watched as they paraded their brilliantly sculpted bodies. He felt a growth in his pants. *Oh no, fuck me.* His dick got hard so fast, he didn't compute he was even aroused before he was fully erect. His entire length, full and ready to fuck. *Down, boy! Down! Ahh, it's no use. He never listens to me.* Ky pushed his erect cock down in an attempt to make it go away. The problem is that it just makes him harder. The only way to rid himself of this was to stroke it until he released the pressure. He looks around to make sure he is alone. *Fuck it. Why waste a good hard on when there is such perfection in front of me.* He unsheathes his aching cock. He palms his length and starts with slow, methodical strokes. He reaches his other hand down to his ball sack and massages it. *Mmmm, these girls look so delicious. God, I wish I could fuck both of them.* He begins to pick up speed. His balance starts to waver, so he takes a step to regain balance. He steps on a branch that snaps, loud enough for the girls to hear during their laughter and splashing.

"Hello?! Is someone there?" Helda calls out, while covering her breasts.

"Come out here, you fucking perv!" Lassia adds.

Fuck. Here we go...

Kysius pulls his pants up over his throbbing cock and adjusts it so it's not so obvious. He steps into the light on the river bank and waves awkwardly.

"Oh, it's you!" Lassia yells.

"Hi. I didn't mean to be a perv, as you so kindly put it," Ky replies.

"He was totally jerking it to us," Helda interjected.

"Were you? Were you touching your little cock to our naked bodies?" Lass asks with a playful tone.

Fuck, this girl is a pain in my ass. She is perfection. Let's try something crazy. Maybe it will shut her up.

Kysius pulls his hard cock out of his pants, as the answer to her question.

"Do you want to come and finish me off?" Ky asks with a cocky grin.

"Are you talking to me or both of us?" Lassia asks while winking at Helda.

"Why choose?" Helda added.

No fucking way. Is this about to happen? Fuck yes! Don't cum quick. Don't cum quick.

Both ladies walk up to the river bank that he is standing on. Helda grabs a downed tree trunk and drags it over to them. *Fuck she is strong. Oh yea, orc, duh.* She drops the log next to him and opens her palm while pointing at it.

"Please, take a seat," Helda says in a joking manner, acting like a butler.

"As you wish," he responds while taking his seat.

Lassia and Helda get on their knees before him and start making out. Lass sticks out her hand and starts rubbing his cock while keeping her lips locked with Helda's. Helda has a hand on his thigh, caressing it. Both ladies have a hand at each other's opening, rubbing and fingering. *Oh fuck, this is so hot.* After a few moments, the girls unlock their lips and turn their attention to Kysius. Lassia bites her lip as she strokes faster and harder, watching his eyes roll back. Helda reaches down and grabs his sack. The girls look at each other before diving onto his genitals. Lassia is licking the tip of his cock taking all his pre-cum on her tongue. Helda is licking and suckling on his balls.

"This is the highlight of my life," Kysius says to the ladies pleasuring him.

"Just wait, big boy. We are only getting started," Lassia replies while stroking his cock. She wrapped her mouth around his cock, barely fitting in her delicate mouth. He had a girthy cock. Helda moved behind Lass to taste her pussy. It was the first time Helda ever had a pussy in her mouth, and she was enjoying it. Lass let out a moan and a whimper.

"Fuck, Helda, you are really good at that. Don't stop!" Lass begged.

Helda giggled and shoved a few fingers in. Lass growled but it was muffled but the massive cock in her mouth. *Fuck, this is so good.* Ky grabbed her by the back of the head and thrust deep into her throat.

"Yea, baby. Take that cock, like a good girl," he growled.

He pulled her head back, releasing his cock from her throat's death grip. Then he pulled her up until she was standing. He positioned her over him and slammed her down onto his cock. *Yes!*

"Oh my, that pussy is so wet and tight," he praised. "Helda, bring that pussy over here." He orders her to stand over his face.

She stood over him. Her height lined up perfectly with his at a seated position, for what was required. She straddled his face and he began to lap her pussy lips. Lass was bouncing up and down on his hard, throbbing cock. She reached out and caressed Helda's ass, which was within reach.

Both women let out moans of pleasure. Kysius had a very skilled tongue. Helda was only sitting on his face for around thirty seconds and she was about to erupt. He reached up and pinched one of her nipples. Just like that, Helda came all over his face.

"Ohhh my fuuuuckingggg Goooodddd" Helda barely says as she releases.

Kysius licked every last drop she had to offer. She dismounted his face and sat next to him on the log. Lassia was still having a blast riding his cock. He lifted her up like a bratty child and placed her on top of Helda.

"Hold this for me and spread your legs," Ky says to Helda.

She did as he instructed. He positioned his rock hard, wet cock between Helda's legs. He brushes the tip of his cock with her clit playfully spanking it. She moaned and bit her lip. Kysius spit on her opening and placed himself inside of her. With long hard thrusts, he made her grunt in pleasure. Meanwhile, Helda's hands are on Lassia's clit and breasts. Occasionally, the ladies would kiss while Kysius was thrusting into Helda. They were all lost in an Eden of sex.

"I think it's time I shared this cock," Ky says with a gentle tone.

He pulled his cock out of Helda and plunged it into Lassia's pussy. Alternating between Lassia and Helda, he was giving them both intentional, hard thrusts. Lassia sounded like she was close. Ky switched to her opening and increased the intensity. She tightened her core and tensed her body. Legs shaking, she came for almost forty seconds.

"Oh my. That was a long one, baby. You like my cock, don't you?" Ky teased.

"Mhmm," she responds while rubbing her aching pussy.

Kysius was already back inside Helda. After making both these girls cum and hearing their moans, he was pretty close himself. He guided the girls to their knees and positioned his cock to reach them both. He stroked his length before these two goddesses and ejaculated ropes of seed all over their beautiful breasts. *Ooooh myyyy, fuuuck yeeessss.* His grunts and growl of pleasure caused vibrations that both women felt all the way down in their pussies.

"Well, that just happened," Kysius says nervously.

"Yea, that was fun," Helda responds.

"It was okay," Lassia says with a devilish wink.

Both girls laughed and ran into the river to wash Kysius off their bodies. *I might as well join them.* He jumps in right after them. The ladies swim to the middle of the river, where it is deep enough to not reach the bottom. The current is weakest at this point in the evening. Kysius swims over and cozies up behind Lassia.

"I have really enjoyed spending time with you today," Ky says with a smile.

"Have you, now?" Lass replies with a smile.

"It doesn't have to end," he added.

"Everything comes to an end," she sighs.

"Not tonight," he says with a wink.

"In the words of a fool, how about you show me?" Lass quips.

Clever girl. Kysius grabbed her and pulled her back to the bank. He stopped in front of the tree trunk they had used just moments ago. Helda can tell this is going somewhere she cannot follow. She gets out and heads back to her tent with an uncontrollable giggle and smile. Crashing into her mouth, their tongues engage in the same seamless dance from earlier in the day. He moves his hand to her opening and massages it. She moans into his mouth. *I love hearing her moan.* His cock gets back to full mast within seconds from hearing her moan. He removes his hand from her pussy and slaps her across the face.

"Ouch! What the fuck?!" Lass asks with an annoyed look.

He slaps her again.

"Dude, what the…" she gets interrupted.

His mouth is on her again. Her anger fades and turns to lust. She will get the hang of it. Kysius pulls back and slaps her a third time. She gives him a smile and licks her lips. *She gets it.* He bends her over the trunk and plunges his cock into her pussy. She lets out a loud moan. He thrusts slowly as he rubs her right butt cheek and under cheek. As he notices the blood has filled the area, he gives it a stern spank. Lassia yelps, followed by a moan. He gives a few more thrusts before delivering another blow to the same spot. Her legs shake and she coats his cock with her cum. Her ass now has a hand print. The blows keep coming and she is reaching her limit.

"Let's find a new spot to make you hurt, real good," Ky says as he caresses her sore ass.

He spanks under her cheek, a much more sensitive spot. She is moaning and drooling from pleasure. Her skin is covered in goosebumps as she cums again. Lass looks drunk with pleasure. She can barely keep herself up.

"I got you, baby," he reassures her.

Kysius held her up with one hand, so she could save her energy for the adrenaline coursing through her body from all the punishment it was receiving. He gives her a couple more blows on her under cheek before deciding to give her a much needed break. He places her on her knees. His cock is coated with all her excitement. She hungrily latches onto it and begins twirling her tongue around his shaft, as she takes all of him. He feels his balls cramping, ready to shoot another load.

"I'm about to cum. Where do you want it, pretty girl?" Ky asks through his teeth.

She spit out his cock and looked up at him.

"I want to swallow your seed, Daddy," she says with her enchanting eyes staring into his.

Those eyes make me melt inside. Fuck, I am so close.

She takes him in her mouth once again. Sucking with more force and bobbing her head with intensity. She maintains eye contact with him the entire time. *Oh no, she looks too good. This feels too good. Fuuuuuck.*

He begins his release and she takes him all the way to the back of her throat. *Oh my god! What the.* She licks the underside of his shaft as he finishes unloading in the depths of her throat.

"I told you, I had a mouth on me," Lass says with a cocky smile.

"That you do, Princess," Ky responds while out of breath.

"I like that you call me princess. No one else does," she admitted.

"Well, you definitely make me want to kneel before you," Ky says with a smirk.

Lassia blushed and giggled at the compliment. They both got dressed and started making their way back to camp. *I really like this girl. There is something more than just lust.*

"Would you like to share a meal sometime? I don't mean Helda. Although she was delicious," Ky asks.

"Oh my god, you are too funny! I have to check my schedule but I might be able to squeeze you in, again!" Lass says with a sexy wink.

I think I am in love. They reached the camp and went to their respective tents. Tomorrow, Kysius needed to pay attention to how the Idyllians worked on getting the Sacred out, so he can plan a sabotage if need be. If only he could get Lassia off his mind for two seconds, to properly execute his plans. Everything hinged on his ability to stall and not give up his true identity.

chapter 9
BRON

It's been days since Kysius left. Bron kept an ear to the ground for any messengers that came back with news from the search party. In the meantime, he tended to his duties at his small bar in the middle of town. His regulars were growing in numbers, ever since the king announced that the Sacred Seven will be brought to the castle. People from all over Ferric were flocking to the town to get a glimpse of it. Bron welcomed the increase in tips, both kinds. He only ever kept one secret from Ky, his sexual preference. In front of his friend, he would flirt with girls and even take them home. Once they were out of sight, he would make up some excuse and let the girl down easy. When he was about fifteen, he realized he only liked boys. It took him a long time to accept it. Bron would force himself to sleep with women to try and change his true desire. It was exhausting and heartbreaking. From the ages of eighteen to twenty-two, it was a vicious cycle of him trying to override his nature. They were the darkest years for Bron. Anytime Kysius noticed his sadness, he would deflect or make up some sob story about how he missed his parents. The truth is that his parents abandoned him when he was twelve. One morning he woke up to an empty house and it stayed that way. Because of this, Bron had no love for his creators. However, it was the perfect excuse to keep Ky off his case. He would wait until Kysius was gone on a quest to satisfy his true sexual desires. This ensured he would not get caught.

Today was the start of the Ruby Festival. The ruby was Ferric's power stone. Similar to the diamond in Idyll, the ruby belonged to the King. It was his source of power and how he maintained it. Unlike the diamond, the ruby was not visible to the public. Thrasus kept it in his castle. He only trusted a select few, in these lands filled with outlaws and rejects. The

Ruby Festival was Kya's idea, Kysius' mother. She thought people should celebrate having such a powerful gemstone in the hands of their ruler and protector. Bron loved Kya. She was the only parental figure in his life after he was abandoned. The boys were only teenagers when she was killed. It brought them closer together. Between losing his mother and his father going on a blood trail, Kysius had no one else to come home to. Many nights were spent drinking and fucking the pain away. Bron was Kysius' home now.

The festival will be extra busy this year. I better make sure we have enough mead and clean mugs. Bron was setting up the bar for the three day festival. The streets were filled with new faces from all shapes, sizes and races. He loved seeing diversity. *Ah, my first customer of the day!*

"Hello there!" he says in a posh accent.

"How's it going, handsome?" replies the ruggedly handsome human gentleman with a country accent, sporting a cowboy-esque outfit.

"It's going great, now that you are here," Bron winks at the stranger.

"Hell, you are too sweet. Would you be so kind as to pour me a pint?" the stranger asks.

"Absolutely. It will cost you though," Bron replies with a tisk in his voice.

"I don't have much, but I am sure we can work something out. What's the damage?" the stranger asks.

"Just your name and a smile," Bron replies.

"Don't make me blush. I am already feeling the heat from this brutal sun. Name is Jayko. What is yours?" Jayko says, followed with a big smile.

Lord help me. What a stud! I wouldn't mind letting this cowboy ride me. Bron turns to hide his ear to ear smile and begins to pour the drink. Jayko's eyes drop to the bartender's muscular ass. Bron turns around and catches him red handed. *He is checking me out. Love that.*

"My name is Bron," he replies.

Jayko bites his lip before taking a sip of his drink.

"Nice to meet you, Bron" Jayko says while tipping his Stetson hat.

The image sends shivers down Bron's spine, causing a twitch below his waist. *I love a sexy cowboy. For the first time in days, I am glad Ky isn't here to cock block me.*

"Are you just passing by? Here for the festival?" Bron inquires.

"I don't care much for festivals or any public event, really. I much prefer to have my own private parties," Jayko says with a devilish grin.

"I am about to go on a quick break. Would you care to join me?" Bron asks.

"You may need to extend your break if I come with you," Jayko says with confidence.

Bron bites his lip and sends a playful shrug to the cowboy that sits before him. He puts up a sign that reads: "Be Back Eventually," and motions Jayko to follow him through the alley. The two good looking gentlemen enter an empty alleyway. Bron turns to Jayko and slams him against the wall, diving into his mouth. They kiss with an impatience that is primal and feral. Jayko is grasping Bron's face as they move their heads around, trying to go deeper. Bron's hands are moving up and down Jayko's body. His fingers keep catching on fabric and lifting his shirt during this exploration of Jayko's body.

"Do you have somewhere we can go?" Jayko asks, through his hot, rapid breath.

"Follow me, cowboy. I hope you are ready for the ride of your life," Bron replies with a face flush from the passionate kiss.

He leads his new friend to his small apartment around the corner from the alley they are in. As they reach the door, the kissing reignites. Jayko begins removing his shirt. Bron mirrors his every move. Both men are stripping down with speed and intention. They are now standing in front of each other totally naked, admiring one another's bodies. Bron is fully hard, the cowboy not so much.

"Let me help you," Bron says, as he licks his lips.

He gets on his knees and maneuvers his mouth to catch the limp cock. He begins to suck on it, willing it to come to life. One hand is placed on Jayko's right thigh and the other is massaging his balls. Bron starts to feel some growth. He twirls his tongue and sucks harder. Moving his lips along the side of the growing cock and cheeking it. As his dick is reaching full length, Bron feels a sharp pain on his back. Jayko was running his nails up Bron's back in pleasure. *I think he is ready for me.* Bron starts kissing his way up Jayko's chest, ending at his lips. The fiery kissing resumes. Making sure the hardwood doesn't go away, Bron keeps stroking Jayko's pretty cock. Jayko moans and his legs start to shake.

"You have me so close. Lay down for me," Jayko demands.

Bron excitedly hops on his bed, on all fours. *I have been waiting so long for this. I need this.* Jayko grabs some rope that is hanging on the wall. He starts tying Bron's hands and feet. *Kinky, I like it.* As he finishes tying up Bron, he starts going through the apartment. *What is he looking for?*

"Can I help you find something?" Bron asks.

"I am just looking for a knife," Jayko replies.

A fucking what?

"Knives are not really my thing. I am more of a cock in the ass, kind of guy," Bron replies nervously.

"It will be fun. I promise," Jayko responds.

The cowboy's cock is back to flaccid. Jayko is trashing the place, searching for something. *What is happening right now? He is clearly not looking for a knife.*

"Where the fuck is it?!" Jayko asks angrily.

"Where is what? Can you please untie me?" Bron pleads.

"The money! Where do you keep all your tip money? I saw you leave the bar with a stack of cash last night," Jayko claims.

"I..I..I can't. It's n..not my money to g…give," Bron says with sadness in his eyes.

"I will fucking beat you until you tell me where it is, faggot!" Jayko lashes out.

God, that fucking word! I hate that mother fucking word! Bron's muscles tense and he manages to make a gap in the poorly fashioned rope handcuffs. He keeps his free hand hidden. Jayko removes his belt slowly while spewing more hateful slurs at Bron. Right as Jayko's hand raises with the belt in preparation for the first blow, Bron springs up and tackles the not so sexy anymore cowboy to the ground. He is much stronger and larger than the cowardly man that is now beneath him. Bron proceeds to punch the assailant in the face, so hard that he goes unconscious. Standing and falling back onto his bed, Bron breaks out into tears. His eyes sting of pain and rejection. *Why can't I just have one good thing? I hate sneaking around. I hate lying to Ky. I hate how it makes me feel, hiding my true self. The one time in months that I have an opportunity and it's not even real.* Streams continue pouring out of him. Bron has only ever been with four men. His desire to find true happiness with another man was burning a hole in his heart. *I'm not sure how much longer I can take this.* This giant, beautiful, man just wants someone to share his love and lust with. Unfortunately, he only ever gets one or the other. Ky shares his love and strangers share their lust. Bron wipes his tears away and steadies his heavy heart. His breathing slows to a normal rate. Time to deal with this asshole. He ties up the cowboy and gets dressed. He picks up the limp body and carries him out to a nearby dumpster. In one motion, he tosses the unconscious man into the dumpster. He wipes his hands as he walks away with his head held high. *Back to the bar, I guess.*

The next two days pass quickly and the bar is very busy. Bron is taking orders and serving drinks. Making small talk when he gets a breather. There are fireworks and music all over town. He is in for a big payday at the end of the festival, after paying the King his hefty tax. That was the money Jayko was after. The King takes fifty percent of all profits from any business in town. All other towns in Ferric pay thirty percent. Bron doesn't complain. He is just happy to have his own place and business. The bar has plenty of regulars to make a decent profit and enough strangers pass through town to supply that income. One of his regulars is a castle guard named Fen that gives him all the rumors and hot gossip. He always looks forward to their chats, especially if it is regarding Kysius.

"Hey Fen, How's it hanging?" Bron asks.

"Low and to the left, old friend," Fen replies with a chuckle.

They share a laugh and Bron serves him the usual. Fen raises his mug towards Bron before downing it in one chug.

"Someone is thirsty!" Bron jokes.

"Ahh! I will need at least four more before I go home. Gotta tell the wife that I leave in the morning," Fen says with a lack of enthusiasm.

"Leave? Where are you going?" a worried Bron asks.

"No word from Kysius. We are sending a bigger search party with extra supplies to either help them or find them," Fen says carefully, fully aware of Bron and Ky's relationship.

Shit! Has it been that long since the last messenger?

"I will keep them coming on the house, on one condition," Bron offers.

"You have my undivided attention," Fen replies with a raised brow and smirk on his face.

"Help me get on the search party," Bron says.

"HAH! You want to come save your boyfriend?" Fen jokes.

"What the fuck did you just say?" Bron replies with fire in his eyes.

"Take it easy, lad. Just joking," Fen winces.

"Just get me a spot and drink your mead, Fen," Bron says with a stern tone.

Fen nods quietly and drinks his second drink. Bron has a flood of emotions. He is annoyed at the joke, his experience from the other day, worried about Kysius, and excited to finally be the one on a quest. *I need to close early tonight so I can prepare.* An hour or so passes and he closes down the bar. He heads home and begins to pack for his journey. He hears a knock on the door. *Who could that be?* Bron has been overly cautious since the incident. He grabbed a knife and leaned against the wall by the door.

"Who is it?" Bron yells

"It's your worst fucking nightmare," a familiar voice responds.

Thrasus?! What the fuck does he want? Bron opens the door to see a cloaked Thrasus at his front step. He moves out of the way to allow the King entrance. *This is weird as fuck.*

"So, this is where you live? Hmm," Thrasus says while looking uncomfortable.

"Sorry, I was not expecting company. It's not much either way. Can't really afford luxury with these taxes," Bron jabs.

"Don't start with this again, Bron. I am simply here to ask you a favor," Thrasus says with lowered shoulders. King Thrasus was not known to show an ounce of weakness. This evening, he looks visibly sad. *This is a first.*

"What could I possibly do for you?" Bron replies with furrowed brows.

"I know you are traveling with the search party tomorrow. My son is out there and I have no clue if he is alive or not. Although you and I don't really see eye to eye, I know you boys are like brothers. You wouldn't be going on this quest if you didn't care for my boy. As for my favor, I want you to make sure he is brought home. Dead or alive, I need my boy back home," Thrasus admits with sadness in his eyes.

"I will do everything in my power to return him," Bron replies with empathy.

"Speaking of power, you will be needing some," Thrasus says as he searches his satchel.

What is he talking about? Thrasus pulls out a ruby fractal. He places the fractal in Bron's hand. Then takes a deep breath in and out. "It isn't going to give you much but it is strong enough for a couple uses. Be sure to save it for when the time is right. I am assuming you know the properties of a ruby?" Thrasus inquires.

"I could use some refreshing. Gemology is not my strong suit," Bron replies while rubbing the back of his head.

"Rubies have love, wealth, wisdom, vitality, and safety properties. It is considered by some to be even more powerful than the diamond. If you need protection or find yourself faltering, grasp the fractal tightly and think about what you want from it," Thrasus instructs.

"Yes, sir. Thank you. I promise I won't let you down," Bron says with pride.

"It's not me you will be letting down," Thrasus says before taking a long pause. "Good luck, young man. Bring my son back and you will have my gratitude." Thrasus then walks out of the apartment.

Did that just happen? I have a fucking fractal now? Ky will never believe this. Fuck.. Ky…I hope he is okay.

Early the next morning, Bron wakes up and heads to the rally point. The search party is huge. He counts at least fifty soldiers. *Hmm, no mercenaries this time.* Bron sees Fen in the crowd and waves. He makes his way over to him.

"Hey, why no mercenaries?" Bron asks.

"The King wants only the best on this one. He doesn't trust mercenaries with this," Fen admits.

A large black orc makes his way to the steps at the castle entrance to gain some more height. He turns to the crowd and begins to address it. "I am Commander Ruv. I will be leading this search party. We have reason to believe Idyllians are at the crash site. Ensure you have all necessary supplies and keep your weapons at the ready."

This is sounding worse by the minute. Bron shakes the negative thoughts from his mind and does one final check in preparation for departure. The convoy begins its march towards the Sacred Seven.

FRACTAL

chapter 10
LASSIA

What a fun night! Kysius is quite the specimen. I never thought I could take an orc dick, but I am pleasantly surprised. Lassia slept better than she had in a long time, even though she could only sleep on her left side. She was still very sore from the spanking the night before. *I am definitely going to have a massive bruise on my ass.* Helda walked into the tent with some salve to help alleviate some of the pain and swelling.

"So, tell me. Was it worth the cauldron sized bruise you are going to have?" Helda asks.

"Oh, fuck yea! The pain is the best part. Every time I feel it, it reminds me of how I got it," Lassia says with a wild smile.

"I am usually the one doing the spanking. Being submissive makes my skin crawl," Helda shares.

"You listened pretty well last night," Lass argues.

"That was hardly a submission. I was just going with the flow and enjoying a new experience. If he tried to spank me, I would've drowned him in my cunt!" Helda remarks.

Both ladies fall into laughter at the image. Helda removes Lassia's pants and starts to apply the salve. She is slow and methodical in her application. Lassia winces. *Ahhh…fuuuuuuck! That hurts so good.*

"Taking it like a champ!" Helda says, noticing her friend is fighting demons to avoid making a sound.

"Mhmm," Lassia lets out.

"You know, last night was my first time with a woman," Helda says nervously.

"I would not have guessed that, based on your performance. I don't think my pussy has ever felt that good," Lassia admits.

"Really? I kind of enjoyed it." Helda says while giving Lassia a bombastic side eye.

"Absolutely! You can eat my pussy any time!" Lassia says with a giggle as she looks at Helda with a wanting eye.

Helda's hand starts moving away from the bruise and towards the inside of Lassia's thigh. *I really hope she is about to do what I think she is going to do.* Helda passes a bandage under her leg and grabs it on the other end, with her hand inside Lassia's thigh. *Oh lord! I got excited for a second there.* Helda pulls the bandage over her bruise and ties it snugly. Lassia lets out a small yelp. *Ouch, bitch!*

"All set. I can do it again tomorrow when this wears off," Helda says.

"Oh...Okay. Thanks, babe," Lassia responds.

Helda leaves the tent and heads to the Sacred Seven to help with the excavation. Lassia falls back on her bed and lets out a big sigh. *I am way too horny. I need to fucking chill. Speaking of which, what is Kysius up to? Bitch! I just said I need to chill. Ugh, I am a thirsty hoe. It is what it is.* Lassia hops up and gets dressed. She starts walking towards Kysius' tent. He is shirtless and sweaty. Grabbing an axe, he chops wood with little effort. His cuts are borderline perfect. *God, is there anything this man can't do?*

"Hey, Kysius!" Lassia yells as she approaches.

"Milady," Ky says in a posh accent as he bows.

"Oh dear. Get up you silly goose!" She snaps playfully.

Is this guy for real? He seems too good to be true.

"You mentioned a meal? My schedule just opened up for tonight, if you are still interested," she offers.

"Let me ask my assistant," Ky replies.

He turns around and acts like he is arguing with someone. It sounds heated. He moves his arms around in protest.

"Are we bears? I didn't think so! It is settled!" Ky yells as he turns back to Lassia. "Okay, I am free. What time did you say?" Ky asks.

"Um… I don't even want to ask. Let's say nine?" Lassia says with a chuckle.

"Please hold," Ky replies. He turns around for a second and has another fake conversation before turning back. "My assistant has just informed me that I am free at nine, however it has to be in my tent. I have a very needy staff that misses me if I leave too long."

Lassia looks around to make sure she didn't miss anything. There is not a person in sight. Kysius turns around and grabs something. He then holds his hand out in front of Lassia. He grabs one of her hands and places a frog in it. *What the fuck!* She moves her hand away, dropping the frog. Kysius' reflexes catch the creature before it hits the ground.

"Why do you have a frog?" she asks frantically.

"He is my assistant, Froggie," Ky says with an appalled expression.

Lassia bursts out into laughter. Ky joins in and places the frog back where he grabbed it from. *This fucking guy. That was one hell of a bit.*

"I was trying to be cute and realized I started to seem crazy," Kysius admits. "And you know what they say. When in doubt, grab a frog."

"What?!" Lassia says before bursting out into even more laughter. "Oh no! I can't breathe. I am going to pee myself. Fuck," Lassia says through her hysterical laughter.

Kysius breaks into laughter. They spend a few moments in blissful joy, laughing at how ridiculous that entire situation was. Slowly, they compose themselves with lingering smiles.

"Tonight. Nine. Food and something else?" Kysius proposes.

"Perhaps," Lassia replies with a sly smile.

"Fucking perhaps… A man's favorite response," Ky jokingly complains.

"Bye, Kysius," Lass says as she waves goodbye.

"Call me Ky," Kysius requests.

"Okay. Bye, Ky. I like it," she says as she walks away.

What a fucking hunk. Play it cool, bitch. Play it cool. Lassia makes her way to the Sacred Seven. She sees Helda working with a group of men. Beside them were the two gemologists studying the rare specimen. Lass walks up to the duo. They are deep in conversation. She realizes it's probably best to not interrupt them and walks around the stone, taking it all in. *It truly is magnificent! I've never seen something so beautiful and powerful.* Lassia hears a noise, almost like music. She looks around for the source before realizing it is coming from the Sacred. Lass leans in closer to verify her suspicion. The sound gets louder. She calls out for Helda.

"What's up, Lass?" Helda asks.

"Do you hear that?" Lassia inquires.

"Hear what, babe?" Helda asks with a furrowed brow

"That sound. It sounds like music, almost," Lass replies.

"I don't hear anything. Are you having a heat stroke? How much water have you had today?" Helda asks while placing her hand on Lassia's forehead.

"No, I haven't had water. But that's not the point! I hear music coming from the Sacred," Lassia snaps.

"I will fetch you some water. Get some shade before you get a headache and get grumpy," Helda orders.

Fucking bitch! How dare she? Okay, she is right. I need water. But still! Bitch, I ain't crazy! She still hears the sound. Lassia places her hand on the gemstone, as she leans in closer. A jolt of energy pulses through her, knocking her off her feet.

"Lass!" Helda yells.

Helda runs to Lassia's side. Lassia is unconscious. She is the only healer and she has no pulse. Helda begins to rock her back and forth in devastation.

"Help!!! Somebody!! Help!!!" Helda screams.

Kysius hears the screams for help and comes sprinting to her aid. He slides in. "What happened?" He asks with a panicked look on his face.

"I don't know. She said she heard music or something coming from the stone. Maybe she touched it?" Helda replies through the tears that started falling from her face.

"Stand back, I got her. Please. Helda, I have her," Ky pleads.

Helda reluctantly lets go of her friend's lifeless body and steps aside. Kysius reaches into his pocket and grasps his tourmaline. He places his other hand on her chest and closes his eyes tightly. "Come on! Fucking work! Come on!" Ky yells.

His gemstone is not made for healing. It won't work on her. He stops for a second to think. He reaches to grab her malachite and places it alongside his tourmaline. Looking up a Helda with eyes full of doubt, he places his other hand on her chest.

"Please work!" Kysius pleads.

Life is slowly returning to Lassia's body.

"It's working!" Helda says excitedly.

Lass' eyes slowly open. She is weak but alive. *What the fuck happened?* Kysius helped her to her feet. Helda ran into her and gave a strong embrace.

"You scared the fuck out of me!" Helda says with tears still stinging her eyes.

"I'm sorry. The last thing I remember was leaning in closer to hear the music and then nothing," Lassia says with confusion in her tone.

"Wait, why are you crying? I just blacked out for a second," Lass asks.

"No, Lass. You were dead. You didn't have a heartbeat," Helda replies.

"Then who brought me back and how? I am the only healer here," Lassia asked with more confusion on her face.

Helda moves her head to indicate the gentleman behind her did. Kysius is standing there, looking like he is bracing for impact. *HIM?!*

"Kysius, you have some explaining to do!" Lass claims.

"I just got lucky. I didn't know what I was doing. I grabbed your malachite and it worked!" Kysius says with his hands up in surrender.

"That is not how that works, Ky. Something tells me you are not who you say you are," Lass accuses.

"Lassia, calm down. You just went through a traumatic experience. Get some rest, we can talk later," he pleads with her.

"No! Guards, arrest him!" Lass orders.

Three soldiers who were spectators to this shit show put Kysius in chains and tie him to the same tree as before. *Mother fucker! I knew he was too good to be true. I need to find out who he really is.* Lassia and Helda head back to their tent to figure out a plan to extract the information she required.

FRACTAL

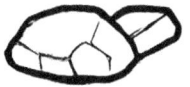

chapter 11
KYSIUS

Note to self: Don't revive Princesses. At least an hour has gone by since he got chained and tied up to this tree, again. He hoped to have a brief stay, as he did the time before. *I need to flirt my ass off to get out of this alive.* Ky was starting to get thirsty and hungry. His dinner date was only a couple hours away but he planned on eating something beforehand. His stomach growled loudly. *Whose dick do I have to suck for some food around here?*

"Guard! Some food and water, please?" Ky yells at the soldier standing a few feet away.

"We were instructed to not let you have anything. Sucks to suck," the soldier says while chuckling.

"I'll suck your dick for some bread," Ky says with a raised brow.

The soldier looks back at him with his mouth ajar, clearly flabbergasted by the remark.

"I'm just kidding, relax soldier," Kysius says before raising his brow again, insinuating he could ,be serious if the situation called for it.

Tough crowd. I guess I will just die of hunger and boredom. I had a good run. Last night was a good send off. Kysius hears footsteps approaching. It's Lassia and Helda coming to interrogate him. Lass dismisses the guards and stands in front of Kysius with Helda at her side.

"Okay, Kysius, if that is even your real name. Who are you and how do you know how to use my gemstone?" Lassia asks.

"My name is, in fact, Kysius. But most people know me as Prince Kysius of Ferric," Kysius says with a comedic tone.

"Are you fucking kidding me?! I fucked the son of the devil himself?!" Lassia says with disgust.

"Excuse you, we had a great time. No need to tarnish the memories,

Princess. Also, my father is no devil. Your mother, however, is pure evil. Hot as fuck, I hear, but a two-faced bitch," Kysius declares.

"First off, STEP mother, dick head. Secondly, she is not evil at all!" Lassia defends.

"I want to thank you for agreeing not to tarnish our memories, very sweet of you. It seems we both like our mommies and daddies, so let's just call it bygones, okay?" Kysius says with wit.

"Ugh, you are infuriating! Can you stop being a fucking clever clown for two seconds?!" Lass says out of desperation.

"Fine. Can you untie me now? I saved your life. You have nothing to fear from me. The worst I can do to you is already on your body," Kysius says as he nudges his head in the direction of her bruised ass cheek.

"No! You are a cruel man from a cruel family, raised in cruel lands," Lassia yells.

"That is rich coming from people that rape and murder innocent women," Kysius bites back.

"What are you talking about?" Lassia asks with an annoyed tone.

"My mother! Idyllic scumbags raped and murdered her without provocation!" Ky screams with tears in his eyes.

"I...I don't know anything about that. That is terrible, Ky. I am so sorry," Lass' tone eases with empathy.

"She was just looking for kazberries, my favorite. They only grow in the midlands once a year. She died because of me! It's all my fault!" Kysius cries out.

"I can't imagine," Lass says with a heavy heart.

"I will never forgive Idyllians for not bringing those men to justice! We sent so many messengers asking for justice. Your stepmother did nothing," Kysius says as he tries to stop the streams leaving his eyes.

"Kysius, no one knew. If those messengers even made it to the Goddess, she never spoke a word of it to anyone," Lassia says and slowly realizes her words.

"You see now. She is evil! I may be able to forgive the unknowing, but never the unwilling," Kysius declares.

"What can I do? How can I fix this? Let me take this hurt away," Lass says while trying to reach for him.

"No!" Kysius bites at her. He jerks his body to repel her touch. "I need to keep this hatred for her. It fuels me. I have to honor my mother's memory!" Kysius growls.

"Do you think she wants you to live out your days full of hate? She would want you to let go and live a full life, free of all this negative energy," Lass explains.

"That may be so but I have my priorities. Forgiving the Goddess is not among them," Ky says as the tears are drying on his face, leaving him flush with anger.

Lassia asks Helda to bring some food and water. She eyes her prisoner with caution, reading his every expression and movement. Her mind stirs with reasons to not trust him again, but she can't help but want to. Helda returns with food. *Oh, thank God. Food!* Lassia grabs the food and begins to feed Kysius. He is lunging at the food like an animal. Chewing quickly and swallowing before he's even finished breaking it all down. *Fuck, this is so good!* Lassia's eyes are wide with surprise at how ravenous he is. She takes a break from the food to give some water to help wash down his barely chewed food.

"Ahhh, thank you. I wasn't sure I would get food or water before dying," Kysius said before taking more bites of the food in Lass' hand.

He finishes the remaining food and drink. Lassia looks into his eyes. They hold a deep gaze for a moment. She places her hand on his face. He pushes his face deeper into her palm and closes his eyes. She feels like home. Helda is watching intently, ready to strike if he tries anything to hurt Lassia. Her friend seems to be entranced by Kysius in his vulnerable state. Lassia can't help but feel empathy and an intense desire to help him heal.

"Is there anything else you can tell me about you? If I find out any more secrets, not from your mouth, you will be stuck back on this tree with no food, no water and no pretty girls to look at," Lassia warns.

"I have told you everything about me. One thing I have not mentioned, however, is that I have my gemstone with me. Just like you have yours, I keep mine with me," Kysius admits.

"Oh?! What kind is it? Wait, don't tell me. I am getting a Citrine vibe from you," Lassia says with enthusiasm.

"It's a tourmaline, Lass," Kysius says with a sad look.

"Oh. I would have never thought that. How do you carry so much pain if you have the best gemstone to heal it?" Lassia asks.

"Because, like I said, I can't let this pain go. I can't let my mother's death go," Kysius says through tired lips.

Lassia nods hesitantly before proceeding to undo his ties and chains. Kysius rubs his wrists, feeling more sore than the last time he was in that position. He looks over at Lassia that is staring back at him. *Those eyes. They make me feel weightless. Is this what love feels like? Am I in love?* He takes a step closer towards her before Helda gets in the way.

"Okay, Kysius. That is close enough for now. Let it breathe, man," Helda says with a stern look.

Kysius raises his hands in surrender and begins to walk backwards towards his tent, never taking his eyes off of Lassia. She was just as invested in that eye contact as he was. Their connection was electrifying. Although it had only been sparked physically, something loomed beneath the surface.

After a long night of sleep, Kysius wakes up feeling like he got a second chance at life. Even though he wasn't the one that died and came back to life, his imprisonment was close enough. *What to do today? Great weather and only two more days until the cavalry arrives. Everything was mostly going to plan. I am still alive and the dig is taking longer than I expected.* Because the military was in charge of setting up the digging schedule and manning, it was not very efficient. Kysius decides to take a stroll around the Sacred to see if progress was made during the night shift. As he approached the dig site, he noticed they had made some decent progress. *Not bad. Maybe I should damage a shovel or two, just in case.* Kysius takes advantage that all the soldiers were on a break and damages one of the shovels by placing it over a rock and stepping on it. *Whoops. Clumsy me.* He kicks the shovel aside and moves closer to the gemstone. He hears a sound, like music. *Is this what Lassia was hearing yesterday? I am not touching that shit!* He listens carefully, trying to make out the sound. It's vaguely familiar. *Where have I heard this before?* Ky racks his brain searching for the answer. *Nothing.* He scratches his head and sighs. Lost in thought, he walks to the river. Hoping the relaxing sound of rushing water will calm his mind. He sees the tree trunk on the riverbank. All the memories of that night come rushing back. His cock twitches. That night was truly amazing. He hears footsteps. *Money, it's Lassia.* Ky turns to see Lassia focused on him and walking directly to him. *Down boy, down. We need to focus on this sound, not pussy.* She reaches him and gives him a sweet smile.

"What brings you to the scene of the crime, big boy?" Lassia says playfully.

"Big boy? You have a good memory, Lassia. I just needed to clear my head," Kysius replies while blushing.

"What's on your mind? I see you are thinking really hard," Lassia says and nudges her head towards his hardened cock.

"Um, yea. That's just always like that," Ky says with a nervous laugh.

"You wouldn't lie to me, would you? I warned you," Lassia says slyly.

"Fine, I was trying to clear my head. But then I saw the tree trunk and my mind got flooded with flashbacks," Ky admits.

"I see. Seems like you are having a hard time remembering," Lassia jokes.

Kysius grins and chuckles under his breath. He looks deep into Lassia's eyes. They are locked in. Her laughter turns to a submissive gaze.

"I think it's time for you to get on your knees," Ky commands.

Lassia gets on her knees while maintaining eye contact. Kysius undoes his pants and lets them fall, freeing his length. Lassia breaks eye contact to marvel at the impressive cock in front of her. He brushes her hair behind her shoulders.

"Suck," Kysius orders.

She wastes no time. Her mouth wraps around his shaft, taking all of him. Slowly working herself back to the tip, she twirls her tongue and applies constant pressure. *Oh fuck! She has the best mouth my cock has ever felt.* She places a hand on his shaft. Ky slaps it away.

"Uh uh. No hands," Ky growls.

She continues enjoying her sweet treat. He grabs hold of her hair, using it to push deeper into her tight throat. He holds her there for a few seconds, making her slap at him. He pulls her head all the way back, his cock completely removed from her delicious mouth. Her face is flush and covered in her own saliva.

"You look so beautiful on your knees, Princess. You are such a good girl," Ky praises.

Lassia lunges back onto his cock, needing more. It wasn't a choice anymore. They needed each other's bodies. No one could satisfy either of them the way they could. It is as if they were made for one another.

"I am so close. Don't stop," Ky pleads.

He lets her ravage his cock for another moment, before pulling its length from her lips and stroking it at his preferred pace.

"Open your mouth, Lass," Ky orders.

She does as he asks and adds a little extra. She sticks her smooth, velvety tongue out. There is saliva dripping from the tip of her tongue. The sight of it drives Ky to the edge. *Ooooohhh fuuuuuuckkk!* His seed shoots out in ropes all over her wanting tongue, mouth, and face. She takes him back in her mouth, gently sucking and licking the last of his cum from his tip. Kysius grabs her face and pulls her up into a kiss. His tongue invades her mouth. He can taste himself, but he likes it. He enjoys tasting her mouth after he claims it. He pulls away, filled with euphoria.

"You are so perfect, Lassia. Truly, perfection," Ky praises.

"You are pretty amazing yourself. Your body is very addictive. I can't get enough," Lass says as she wipes the side of her mouth with her thumb.

Lassia starts to get dressed. Kysius puts a hand up, motioning her to stop.

"What are you doing? It's your turn, Princess," Kysius says.

"I'm good, Ky. I like being your little slut. Let me keep this feeling. Save it for later," Lass replies with a wink.

Lassia finishes getting dressed and blows him a kiss before walking away. *I am definitely in love. Fuck. Oh shit! The sound. I lost it. Fuck. Ahhh, I will deal with it tomorrow. I need some food after that. I am starving!*

chapter 12

HELDA

Myka has been obsessed with me ever since I fucked his brains out. I expect nothing less. Sure, I enjoyed him but he is a little coward. I can't be with someone like that but like Lass said, a little fun never hurt anyone. That bitch is a bad influence but I love her. Helda has been avoiding Captain for days. She relishes in his continued attempts to get her attention. He is persistent and determined to have her again. He may even want something more. Helda decides that today she will play with her toy. The events of yesterday had her stress and emotions at an all-time high. She has some sexual tension built up from rubbing the salve on Lassia's butt cheek. *What can I bring that would make this more fun?* Helda grabs a couple items and puts them in a satchel. She heads out to find Myka. The Captain is at his tent, looking over the digging schedule. Helda stands at the entrance.

"Permission to enter, Captain," she says in a deep, manly voice.

"Come in, soldier," Myka responds without taking his eyes off of the schedule.

"You always let people enter your tent without looking? I could've been an assassin," Helda says in her normal voice.

"O..oh h..hey Helda. W..What are you doing in my tent?" he stumbles over his words and the bench behind him.

"I was in the area and decided to drop by. See how my little Captain was doing," she said in a playful tone.

"O..okay. Well, can I get you anything? Are you thirsty? Oh, I have wine!" Myka offers with a slight panic in his voice.

"Oooh, you have wine? Don't mind if I do," Helda replies with a grin.

The Captain fumbles around his belongings and manages to find two cups. She sits on his bed and places her satchel down. He grabs the wine and pours it onto the cups, before handing one to Helda.

"This isn't poisoned, is it?" Helda pokes fun.

"I would never poison you! That would be a waste of your beauty." Lutrix replies with a smitten smile.

"Good," Helda replies as she takes a long drink.

Fuck, this is good wine! She puts the cup down and removes her top, exposing her breasts.

"It's so hot in here," she says as she winks.

"Y..Yes. I..It is," Myka struggles to speak the words.

She fans herself a bit and takes a few more drinks. Pushing her breasts together with her arms, she looks up at a dumbfounded Captain Lutrix.

"You okay there, Myka?" she asks with a devilish smile.

"Mhmm," is all he manages to get out.

"Well, Captain, this has been nice. But I must take my leave. Duty calls," she says as she puts her top back on.

"W..Wait. You've only just arrived. Can I offer you more wine?" he offers.

"I have to go, Myka. We can have another glass some other time," she responds.

Helda stops at the entrance, turns around, and blows him a kiss. Her eyes fall upon his hardened cock as he stands there, mouth ajar. *Fuck it's hard to pass that up. But, no! I want him to beg.* She leaves the Captain wanting and heads back to her tent without her satchel. *If he is a good boy, he will see my satchel and bring it back.* Helda sat in her tent for some time, waiting for Myka to come by. No sign of him. She figured he got busy and hadn't noticed the bag by his bed. Having grown bored of waiting, Helda goes out in search of Lassia. *I know exactly where that bitch is.* She heads to Kysius' tent. In it she finds Lassia and Kysius, but they were not having sex nor making out. They were playing a card game. *This is interesting. I will let them be. Time to see where my bad boy is.* She walks over to Myka's tent. As she approaches, she notices there is no one there. *Hmmm, where could he be? She looks behind the tent, where she caught him last time. Nothing.* She moves over to the river, the dig site and some of the other soldiers' tents. No luck. He was nowhere to be found. Strange. She decides to head back to her tent with a cloud of disappointment. Everyone she wanted to spend time with was either busy or missing. As she gets close to her tent, she notices her sachet at the entrance. She picks up speed and grabs the bag, all the items still inside. Then she hears a man clearing his throat from inside the tent. Her head snaps to see who it is. It's Captain Lutrix.

"Helda, I wanted to bring back your bag. You left it by mistake in my tent," he says sweetly.

"It wasn't a mistake," she basically growls.

She lunges towards him, crashing her lips onto his. He moans in delight of what she is gifting him with. Helda is sitting on his lap, straddling him. She removes her shirt and returns to his lips. She bites his bottom lip and pulls back on it. He growls and returns the favor. *He is a good boy.* She grabs his face and places his mouth on her left nipple. He licks around the areola and teases her nipple with soft bites. Occasionally sucking as much of her breast as he can fit in his mouth. *Fuck that feels good!* He mirrors the pattern on her right nipple.

"More!" Helda demands.

He increases his suction on her right nipple while pinching and squeezing the other. Helda's sensitive nipples are a straight shot to her pussy. *Oh my god, I am close.* She can feel his pulsing hard cock. It's making her so wet.

"Don't stop, Myka. Don't you fucking dare stop!" she cries out.

The Captain swaps his mouth and hands to the opposite nipples. Within seconds she is shuddering and releasing her creamy goodness all over his lap. She stands up and puts her shirt back on.

"What about me?" Myka asks with a cocky smile.

"What about you?" she replies with a raised brow.

"I am hard as a rock. What am I supposed to do with this?" Myka asks with a confused look on his face

"I don't know. Go ask one of your soldiers to suck you off," she jabs.

"Helda, please. I only want you. I haven't been with anyone since that amazing night with you. Please. I will do anything," he begs.

"Anything? Okay, take your pants off and bend over like the good boy you are," she commands.

"Y..yes, ma'am," he obeys.

Myka removes his pants, exposing his large erect cock, already dripping pre-cum. He bends over as she requested. *This will be fun.* Helda grabs a rope from her satchel. She has one end frayed and a monkey fist knot on the other end. She starts by using the frayed side, striking his ass. Myka winces in pain but steadies himself. Let's see how much this soldier can take. She strikes him again in the same spot. No reaction this time. Helda strikes two more times, back to back, in the same spot. No real reaction. *Okay, buddy. Let's see how you handle a monkey fist.* She turns the rope around and lands a blow, right on his under cheek. Lutrix lets out a muffled scream. He felt that one. She moves to the other side of his butt and delivers the same blow. Another muffled scream escapes Myka's mouth. His body is shaking from the adrenaline. His cock has softened. His breathing is labored. Maybe I should give him a little bit of pleasure before doing more. She reaches between his legs and grabs his semi-hard cock and begins to stroke. Her free hand is rubbing the sore spots. She feels him hardening again. Helda dives her face into his ass and starts licking his asshole. The Captain lets out the most intense moan his body could ever muster. She is lapping and circling his tight hole and she strokes him faster and harder. His body has changed from shaking to tightening. She feels his cock throbbing and his balls pulling. He is about to cum. Helda stops everything. Leaving him on the edge, aching and throbbing. There is so much pre-cum, you would think he actually came.

"Why?! Why did you stop? It felt so good and I was so close," Myka complains.

"I am not done playing with you, Captain," she responds.

His head falls in disappointment. Suddenly, he feels something enter him. He lets out a groan. Helda just put a candlestick in his ass.

"Don't move. We don't want it to break off in there," she orders.

She moves over to the side where his head is, candlestick still in his ass. He looks up to meet her gaze and is met with a hefty slap to the face. *Why is this so satisfying? I don't like hurting people. This is different, though.* He keeps his mettle. She backhands him this time. He growls at her and she rushes in to kiss him. *He is so good for me.* She moves back behind him and removes the candlestick. Myka gasps and moans. She throws the candlestick to the side and flips him over. She removes her pants and sits on his longing cock. It doesn't take much for him to get back to the edge. He reaches his hands up and grabs her breasts and she grinds on his length. His toes curl in an effort to hold his orgasm, but the pleasure is too great. He erupts inside of her. *Oh, I can feel his yummy cum in my pussy.* She slows her grinding, allowing him to fully release. His arms drop to his sides as he lays in exhaustion. She stands up and gets dressed.

"Take all the time you need, Captain. I am going to wash off in the river. Thank you for being my good boy," she smirks.

She leaves him naked, exhausted, and satisfied in her tent. Helda has the biggest sense of pride and accomplishment consuming her. Being a domme is a new discovery that she is very much enjoying.

chapter 13
LASSIA

The long awaited date was finally happening. Lassia and Kysius decided to have a meal, shortly after their little run-in at the river. She walks up to his tent and is pleasantly surprised. He managed to make some branches into a table and a pair of stools. A pelt is draped over the makeshift table and each stool has a pillow to sit on. In the center of the table are a handful of flowers. She catches him watching her with the corner of her eye.

"I see you creeping," Lassia calls him out.

"I call it admiring," Ky replies.

Lassia blushes and turns to hide her amusement. Kysius brings out two mugs with wine. *Wow, what a gentleman. He did all this for me? How sweet!* Kysius pulls out her stool and motions her to sit. She takes her wobbly seat and is handed her wine. *Oh my god, I am going to break this thing.*

"Don't worry, you won't break the stool. It just needs to settle," Kysius says with a comedic tone.

"Oh, so you are a mind reader now?" Lassia retorts.

"Depends, are you thinking about fucking me right now?" Ky asks.

Yes, one hundred percent, yes. Bend me over right now!

"Perhaps," she says taking a drink of her wine to hide her smile.

Kysius hums with a raised brow. He moves to his own stool and takes a seat. The moment he puts weight on the branches, they give out, making him fall on his ass and spilling wine all over him. *Holy shit!* Lassia erupts in laughter. Kysius slowly gets back to his feet with a laugh of his own.

"I'm sorry. I don't mean to laugh at you. I just find it hilarious when people fall," Lass apologizes with scattered laughter.

"It's fine. It is quite comical," Kysius responds.

"Indubitably," she agrees in a posh accent.

"You say 'indubitably,' too?" Kysius asks with a smile.

"Indubitably," she responds again in a posh accent.

"Touché," he says with a posh accent.

Kysius grabs the bundle of sticks that were supposed to be his stool and tosses them aside. Lassia is enjoying her wine as she watches this vision of manhood being a mess trying to impress her.

"How did you get wine?" she asks.

"Captain Lutrix keeps a few bottles in his tent. I swiped one when he wasn't looking," Ky responds with an evil grin.

"You naughty boy!" she jokes.

"I don't have to tell you," he insinuates.

His words spark memories of their naughty moments. *Fuck, did it just get hot in here? Whew!* She takes a long drink of her wine, nearly finishing it off. Kysius' eyes go wide.

"Everything okay there, Lass? Got thirsty, huh?" Kysius says in a cocky tone.

"Shut up," Lassia says with little care in her words.

Kysius throws his hands up in surrender and chuckles. They enjoy their meal, with Kysius sitting on a rock he found nearby. As they finish, Lassia brings out a deck of cars. Time to see if this guy is a good liar.

"The game is called Bullshit. Have you played it?" Lass inquires.

"A time or two. Remind me of the rules," Ky replies.

"The entire deck is dealt to the players. The youngest person goes first. The first player must play aces, face down, in the middle of the table. Even if they don't have any, they must play at least one card and say it is an ace. You can play as many cards as you want and it doesn't have to be the actual cards you are saying it is. If someone calls bullshit and you lied about what you put down, you pick up all the cards in the center. After aces, the next person must play twos. It goes all the way to king, then back to ace. The first person to run out of cards wins," Lassia explains.

"Thank you for that very elaborate explanation," Ky says with a smile.

"Are you ready, then?" Lassia asks.

Kysius nods. Lass deals the cards and looks at her hand. *I have a pretty solid hand.*

"How old are you? I am twenty four," Lassia says.

"I am twenty seven. I guess you go first," Ky replies.

An older man? I love that. I knew he was, but it's nice to have confirmation. Lassia starts with an ace and a four. Kysius looks at his hand and says nothing. He places one two down. *He is playing it safe. Interesting.* Lassia clears her throat and places two threes down. Ky opens his mouth, then shuts it while blowing air through his nose. He thinks for a moment before playing his next turn. Into the center, he plays a four and a five. Lass quickly plays her turn, putting down two fives and a jack.

"Bullshit!" Kysius yells, peeking over the cards in his hand.

"Fuck," Lass lets out a sigh in disappointment.

They both laugh as she collects all the cards in the middle.

"My turn!" Kysius says as he resumes the game.

They played for hours, getting to know each other in the process. Many in the camp heard their laughter and the occasional "Bullshit!" Eventually, one of the soldiers came over to ask them to lower their voices. They offered their sincerest apologies and continued their evening with a more respectful volume. At midnight, Kysius grabs a blanket and Lassia's hand and guides her to a spot outside the encampment.

"Where are we going, Ky?" Lass asks with a smile.

Please tell me he is finally going to fuck me. I have been wet for the past two hours. I need some dick!

"Do you trust me? Just wait," Ky assures her.

They reach a patch of shorter grass and he lays the blanket down. He lays down and Lassia pounces on top of him. Her lips crash into his. Her ravenous tongue pushes into his mouth and he welcomes it. She starts to feel his cock stiffening. He carefully pushes her away and moves her to lay next to him. *What? Why is he stopping me?* He takes a deep breath and rearranges his hard cock. He clears his throat and combs his hair back with his hand.

"I'm sorry, Princess. That's not why I brought you here," Ky says.

"Oh. Why did you?" Lass asks with furrowed brows.

"I really like you. More than just sexually. I feel a strong connection to you and I think you feel it, too. I wanted to see if I could just be with you without sex and still enjoy it. I have never been able to do that with anyone," Ky nervously admits.

Oh my god, that is incredibly sweet. My heart.

"Perhaps. I am willing to try this experiment with you," Lass replies sweetly.

Kysius pulls her into his chest. She cuddles up to him. They lay there, watching the stars fill the night sky. A wave of peace and comfort washes over them. *I can get used to this.* Lassia looks up at Kysius and he catches her gaze. They share a gentle kiss and return to their cuddling. Sleep finds the lovers laying in a field.

The morning sun shines on the couple. Lassia wakes up with no Kysius in sight. *Where did he go?* She gets up and grabs the blanket. She heads back to Ky's tent to find him shirtless cooking breakfast. *Oh my! I don't know what I am more hungry for.* Lass catches his eye and he lets out a big smile. She approaches him and plants a kiss on his cheek.

"Last night was really nice," she says delicately.

"It was the best night of my life," Kysius lets slip. He slaps his hand over his mouth in disbelief that he just said that out loud. "Shit! I didn't mean to say that out loud," Ky says nervously.

"Relax. It was pretty amazing," Lassia says as she caresses him.

Her hand moves from one shoulder to the other, dragging it across his back. His skin breaks out into goosebumps. *He likes it. Men really are just boys who want love and attention. Tough on the outside but mush on the inside.* Kysius hands her a plate of food and they sit to enjoy breakfast. Smiles and insinuating looks are being thrown around. *He better be careful with those looks. Mama wants some attention.* She places her hand on his lap. She notices his cock twitch. Lass bites her lip and looks up at him with those fuck-me eyes. Ky chuckles.

"Uh uh. Eat your breakfast, Princess. You are going to need your strength for later," he urges.

"What is happening later?" Lass asks with a grin.

Kysius shrugs and throws her a wink before returning to his meal. *This man.* Lassia giggles with excitement and continues to eat. As they are cleaning up their plates, they hear a man yelling near the Sacred Seven.

"It's ready!" a man yells.

"Oh shit!" Ky lets out.

"What was that?" Lassia asks.

"Uh, nothing," Ky replies.

chapter 14

BOTUK

All of Kysius' men are waiting for the reinforcements to arrive at the rally point. Botuk has taken the role of the leader, bestowed by Kysius. Most of the mercenaries like this decision. The few that did not agree were too scared to do anything about it. Chances of a mutiny were slim to none. The only issue the group of men were facing was the lack of supplies. They did not get a chance to stock the rally point, due to the lack of supplies in the main encampment. When they retreated, there was no time to take any supplies. It fell to Botuk to figure out a solution. *I miss only taking care of myself. This leader shit is not for me.* He calls a meeting to figure out a plan.

"How is the hunting going?" Botuk asks.

"It's been rough, boss. All the good hunting is too close to the crash site," one of the mercs replies.

"What about fishing? We can still access the river without getting close," Botuk suggests.

"Waters are too murky to spear and we have no bait to use a pole," another merc replies.

"Let's keep looking for good hunting spots. We need food soon." Botuk orders. "Kysius said his army should be here in the next couple of days. Start rationing food until we get a good hunt."

I can't wait for these reinforcements to get here, so they can take over. I still need to figure out how to explain who I am and how I became the leader without them killing me.

"Who here has a good relationship with Commander Kruil? Kysius said he would likely be the one in charge of the reinforcements," Botuk inquires.

"I do," Espacio says.

"Well, if it isn't the frying pan of death, himself," Botuk jabs.

"Yea, yea. Let it all out, troll. Make fun of an old man," Espacio jokes back.

"I need you to be the first person to interact with the reinforcements commander. Let him know I am in charge by Kysius' orders. I don't want to cause a scene when they see me," Botuk expresses.

"I got you, boss," Espacio assures.

Botuk had a fairly good relationship with Espacio in the short period of time that they knew each other. He was relieved to have him be the answer to his prayers. With the plan figured out, the meeting was adjourned. The mercenaries seem to be content with how the meeting concluded. Botuk makes his way to his corner of the rally point and plops down. He places his club beside him and closes his eyes for the night.

Sounds of men yelling wake Botuk. The sun is already high in the sky. *Shit, I slept pretty hard. What's all that commotion?* Botuk grabs his club and gets to his feet. He sees a large group of soldiers almost to the rally point. Finally, backup has arrived. He makes his way to the outskirts of the rally point, avoiding detection. Botuk must now lie in wait for Espacio to give the all clear. He watches as the army of soldiers melds with the group of mercenaries. Espacio is talking to a large black orc. That must be Commander Kruil. Some time passes and he hears Espacio banging his frying pan with a wooden spoon. There is the signal. Botuk makes his way to their position. As he approaches, he can see Kruil examining him with a hint of arrogance on his face.

"You must be Commander Kruil. Kysius told me you would be coming and boy am I glad you are here," Botuk says with a sigh of relief.

"A troll, huh? I've never seen one before. I thought you would be bigger," Kruil says in a snobby tone.

"Is that what ladies say to you, back home?" Botuk jabs.

"What did you say?!" Kruil snaps.

"Relax, little one. Don't be so sensitive," Botuk jokes.

"I will gut you!" Kruil threatens.

"Okay. Can we not do the whole bigger dick thing? I am too hungry and you don't want me kicking your ass in front of your friends," Botuk says with a sigh.

Commander Kruil huffs and puffs, before letting out an annoyed groan. He looks around and straightens his back.

"What is your name, troll?" he asks with reluctance.

"Botistanuckashuk," Botuk replies.

"What do your friends call you?" Kruil inquires.

"Botistanuckashuk," Botuk says with a serious face.

"Okay then. Botilisacanuk, does Prince Kysius have a plan?" Kruil asks.

"Botistanuckashuk," Botuk insists.

"Botistanuckalaka," Kruil fails to pronounce.

"Botistanuckashuk," Botuk says, slower this time.

"Botistanuckashuk," Kruil says with a confused face.

"Yes. Now what was the question?" Botuk pokes fun at the Commander.

"Ugh," Kruil sighs in defeat.

"Just kidding. Come, let's talk over a drink. You brought mead, yes?" Botuk says while putting an arm around Kruil.

They go over the plan Kysius laid out. The mead has done a number on all the men. Both parties decide it is best to advance on the dig site tomorrow. The arrival of food and alcohol has the mercenaries and the tired soldiers welcoming a night of relaxation and indulgence. The two leaders have joined the rest of the men in the festivities, having concluded their briefing. A tall handsome human walks up to Botuk and taps him on the shoulder.

"Excuse me. I hear that you are the one in charge of Kysius' men," the man states.

"I was. This is Big Dick Kruil's party now," Botuk says with a smile and a chuckle while shoving Kruil's shoulder.

"Is he okay? Why did you guys leave him?" the man asks with a hint of anger.

"Whoa! Easy there, human. Who are you?" Botuk asks with furrowed brows.

"My name is Bron. I am his best friend. I came to help, by order of King Thrasus," Bron says with pride.

"Well, I am his best friend. So, you must be an imposter," Botuk replies jokingly.

"We have a comedian! I see why he likes you. But seriously, what the fuck happened?" Bron asks with less intensity.

Botuk fills Bron in on how the event unfolded. He does his best to ease Bron's mind. *This guy really is his best friend. Loves him like a brother. Maybe if I go back with them, they will love me, too. That would be nice.* Botuk makes an effort to make Bron like him. After all, Bron is best friends with Botuk's only friend. The night continues with more drinking and relaxation. Botuk and Bron have spent the night joking and playing drinking games. Botuk ventures off into the treeline for a quick pee break. Bron follows closely behind. As Botuk begins to relieve himself, he hears footsteps behind him. He cuts off his stream and turns to face the invader. Bron throws his hands up in surrender.

"Whoa, big fella! I am just coming here to do the same," Bron says in his defense.

Botuk relaxes his tense shoulders. His cock is still out as he stands in front of a frozen Bron. Bron's eyes are glued to Botuk's cock. *Is he staring at my dick?* Bron undoes his pants and unsheathes his girthy cock. *Shit! That's a thick cock.* Bron is already semi hard. Botuk's cock twitches at the sight of it. *What the fuck?! Why am I getting hard right now?* Bron notices the troll is filling out his length. He moves closer. *Fuck! What should I do? Why am I not stopping this?* Bron closes the last of the distance between them and grabs Botuk's massive cock. *Oh! That actually feels good. Why do I want to grab his?* Botuk reaches down and grabs Bron's dick. This feels so nice, actually. They both start to stroke each other. Hot breath and grunting is all you can hear. Bron pulls Botuk by the cock and places their cocks together. He slaps Botuk's hand away and uses both his hands to stroke the cock sandwich he created. *OMFG! This feels incredible.*

"Are you ready to cum, big guy?" Bron asks.

"Wha…?" Botuk tries to reply.

Before Botuk could finish his question, Bron spits on their cocks and strokes faster. *Fuck!* Within seconds, they are both spewing ropes of cum. The men are covered in a combination of their seeds. Bron releases the dicks and they separate.

"I am fucking dizzy. What the fuck just happened?" Botuk asks in a daze.

"Just some bigger dick stuff," Bron jokes.

The men laugh and clean themselves off. Bron comes up behind Botuk and slaps him on the shoulder. "That was fun. See you in the morning."

"Yea. L…Later!" Botuk responds.

The fuck? That was pretty epic. I really need to pee now. Botuk lets his stream flow with a loud sigh of relief and satisfaction.

CHAPTER 15
KYSIUS

Kysius and Lassia head to the dig site to see what the soldier meant by 'ready.' As they get closer, they see all the workers leaving coming out of the hole they dug. The Sacred Seven is completely unearthed. The Captain had doubled the shifts overnight to get it done quicker. *Fuck!* He must know reinforcements are coming. A few feet away from the stone, Lassia holds her head and whimpers.

"Hey! What's wrong?" Kysius says as he walks towards her.

OOOOOwwww, fuck! He is now standing next to her experiencing the same thing she is. Kysius grabs Lassia and moves them out of the range of the high pitched frequency. The dirt was helping dampen the intensity. Only Kysius and Lassia are being affected by the stone. Everyone else is just staring at them with confused looks on their faces. One of the gemologists walks over to them and asks them what the noise sounded like. They have been studying all of the Sacred Seven's properties for days but this was one thing they could not record.

"Imagine a very high pitched flute with a wavering tone," Kysius says while holding his right ear and wincing.

"That is scary accurate," Lassia adds.

The gemologist rummages through his notes and hums. Ky and Lass just stare at him.

"I got nothing. I will annotate it and do more research when we get this baby home," the man says.

Oh shit! I almost forgot about that. What the fuck am I going to do? Breaking shovels won't help me now. Kysius makes sure Lass is okay before leaving her side. He goes to one of the miners and has some small talk. Eventually, he gets the information he is fishing for. He goes to Helda in hopes he can convince her to help him with his new plan. Plan D, save Lassia and then take the Sacred home to Papa.

"Helda, my darling. May I have a word?" Ky asks.

"Make it quick. We have a lot of prep to do for this transport," Helda replies.

"That is kind of what I need to talk to you about," Ky counters.

"What? You aren't even a part of this," Helda argues with a laugh.

"You won't be transporting this rock anywhere. There is an army on its way here. They could be here any minute. I need you to take Lassia back home tonight. Please, Helda," Ky begs.

"What are you talking about? How do you know this?" Helda inquires.

"It's my army. When my men retreated, it was to wait for backup. My job was to stall you guys, but then I fell in love with Lassia and I can't live with myself if anything happens to her," Kysius admits.

"What the fuck, Ky?! This is so fucked up!" Helda spouts.

"I know, I know. It's all fucked. I need you to take her. Right now," Ky demands.

"Fine. But just know she will never forgive you for this," Helda says.

"I know. I hate this, but it is what it is," Ky says with defeat in his voice.

Lassia is watching him the entire time he talks to Helda and walks to his tent. She can tell he is acting strangely and heads to confront him about it. Ky is sitting on his bed, deep in thought. *Fuck! Fuck me! Classic! I finally find the perfect woman and I already fucked it up. I am just destined to be alone.* Lassia walks in, in the middle of his self-deprecation session. She notices his distraught face.

"What's wrong Ky? You are scaring me. I saw you talking to Helda. It didn't look too good," Lassia says with sadness in her eyes.

"I..I can't even look you in the eyes right now. I am so ashamed," Ky admits.

"Why? What are you ashamed of?" Lass asks with a worried tone.

"I deceived you. I sabotaged your progress on the Sacred to allow time for my army to come and take the Sacred. Of course, I end up falling in love with you. Now I have to lose you. It is all so fucked up," Ky confesses.

"What?! When will they be here? You sabotaged us?" Lass asks with fire in her eyes.

"Any minute now, a legion of Ferric soldiers will overrun this camp. I told Helda to take you home away from this place. I know I can't have you but I need you to be safe. Go to her. Run far from here. Please," Ky pleads.

"I can't believe you, Ky. I was finally trusting you. It was all bullshit," Lass says with tears in her eyes.

"It wasn't bullshit. I love you, Lassia. I have never loved anyone, until you," Ky says while struggling to fight back tears.

Lassia can't bear the words she is hearing. She turns away from him and sobs uncontrollably. Ky moves to console her but she evades his touch and leaves. *Fuck! I feel so much pain. Why does it hurt so much? This is worse than torture.* Kysius is experiencing heartbreak for the first time since he lost his mother. He grasps his tourmaline and does his best to cleanse himself but it has no effect. Fuck this useless thing! He tosses it aside. Nothing he does seems to ease the pain. *I know what can rid me of this pain. New pain.* He reaches for his tourmaline and places it on his left shoulder. Kysius has never used his gemstone on himself before. He doesn't know what damage it could cause, he also doesn't care. With his eyes closed tightly, tears still piercing through, he unleashes the power of his stone. *AAAAaaahhhhhh! Fuck!* The burst of energy seared a hole in his shoulder, cauterizing as it burned through. This is definitely a distraction. *Fuck, this hurts!* He manages to balance his pain from the heartbreak with the pain from the new crater in his shoulder. However, the intensity of the pain makes him pass out on his bed.

Kysius wakes up the next morning with an immense ache in his shoulder and a massive headache. *Shit! Lass!* He pushes through the pain and runs to see if the ladies left. To his relief, they were gone. *Oh, thank God! Also, ouch. I miss her.* His eyes start to pool. He wipes away the unwelcome tears and sniffs loudly, trying to regain composure. A commotion by the gemstone catches his attention. He focuses his still half-awake eyes to see his army fighting the Idyllian soldiers. There is a sight for sore eyes, pun intended. He makes his way to his tent to freshen up before greeting his men. I don't need people asking me about the crater in my shoulder or my red eyes. Kysius, Prince of Ferric, is now in full character. He makes his way over to the Ferrican's that have already concluded their skirmish. There are a few Idyllian soldiers in chains, Captain Lutrix being one of them.

"There he is! Prince Kysius!" Commander Kruil says as he dawns a salute.

All the soldiers snap to attention and present their salutes. Kysius returns the salute and everyone retracts theirs. Ky walks over to Kruil and gives him a hearty handshake that gets pulled into a hug.

"I am so happy to see you, Kruil. I hope the journey wasn't too bad,"

Ky says.

"Ahh! Smooth sailing. I did bring you something from home," Kruil says with a smile.

Bron emerges from underneath the crowd. Kysius' eyes widened with surprise. Bron runs into Kysius' arms with a mighty embrace. *Man, I have missed my brother!* They separate when a large shadow is cast over them. *I know what throws that kind of shade.* Kysius looks up to see his beloved troll friend, Botuk.

"Come here, you big brute!" Ky yells.

"Fuck you, brute!" Botuk jabs back as they share an embrace.

Kysius is standing in front of his entire army with the Sacred Seven prepared for transport back to Ferric. *I love it when a plan comes together.* His eyes scan the army, his friends, the stone and then fall to Captain Lutrix. *What to do with this one?*

"Captain Lutrix. If I remember correctly, you had me chained and tied to a tree. Twice, mind you," Kysius says playfully.

"I…I only did it o..once. The Pri.." Lutrix pleads.

"Enough!" Ky interrupts him before he mentions the Princess.

"You will be chained and tied to the same tree you so graciously attached me to. And if you so much as make a sound, you will be gagged," Ky orders.

Soldiers take the Captain away in chains. Kysius looks at the remaining prisoners and prepares to give them options. He is a big fan of pirates and follows their code. Join or die. All of them chose to join. Smart choice. *Arrr. Now the real fun begins getting this fucking massive rock back home.* The Idyllian plan was not terrible, but that is one massive rock. Ky calls for a meeting with his gemologists. The rest of the men are preparing for supper and getting some much earned rest.

"Give me options, gents. We need this thing moved and I don't think we have the necessary horsepower to move it," Kysius says with a chuckle at the end.

"Very good pun, sir. You are correct. There is no way to efficiently transport the gemstone in its current form. However, if we could fracture it into smaller pieces, it can be transported with ease," Espacio recommends.

"Fracture it? Won't that weaken the gemstone? My dad would be pissed," Ky asks.

"We have read about Sacred Sevens being fractured and melded back together with a stone of similar quality," Espacio adds.

"Are you saying we can use the ruby?" Ky inquires.

Espacio nods with approval. This is great news! Kysius gives his approval and the gemologists exit. Left on his own for the first time since his army arrived, he begins to feel the weight of his heartbreak. *Oh no. I don't want to think about how much I miss her. Why? Why must it haunt me?* He realizes that using his tourmaline to escape his heartbreak is a bad idea. It causes more hurt and doesn't really rid him of the problem. Kysius hears footsteps and quickly tries to act normal. Bron and Botuk walk into his tent.

"Hey guys! How's it going?" Kysius says with a small sniffle.

"What's wrong, dude? Were you crying?" Bron asks with a furrowed brow.

"No! Shut up, loser!" Ky says before throwing a punch at his friend's shoulder.

"Fuck you, dude!" Bron replies and punches Ky back, the one with the crater.

Fuck me, dead! Kysius does everything in his power to hold back the pain. He inflates his cheeks with air and slowly lets the air out. Bron gives him a strange look.

"I didn't hit you that hard, bro," Bron says as he blows raspberries at Botuk that is laughing in the corner.

"How did the meeting go?" Botuk asks, trying to contain his laughter.

"It went. We are going to break the stone and put it back together when we get home, using the ruby," Ky informs the boys.

"Sounds dumb," Botuk scoffs.

"Oh shit! Look what your dad gave me," Bron says as he pulls out the ruby fractal.

"No fucking way! He gave you a fractal? He never let me have one. This is bullshit!" Ky says in joking annoyance.

Bullshit... Fuck. Lassia... He will forever think of Lass any time he hears, thinks or speaks the word 'bullshit.' Sadness overcomes him. He can't hide it anymore.

"Okay, man. What the fuck is your deal?" Bron interrogates.

"I fell in love with the fucking Princess of Idyll and I had to let her go so she wouldn't get killed or force me to show weakness in front of the men," Kysius comes clean.

"What the fuck?!" Bron and Botuk say, almost in unison.

"Was she hot?" Botuk asks.

"Shut up! I need all the details but first, let me grab some mead and some bread. Tonight just got so much more interesting," Bron says with a giddy smile.

"Great. Now I have to relive all my memories of the woman that I will never see again," Ky complains.

"Yea, but was she hot though?" Botuk insists on asking.

"The most beautiful, sexual, caring, funny, and challenging woman I have ever met. So, yes buddy, she was very hot," Ky reminisces.

Bron returns with a keg of mead that he rolled all the way from the wagon and a bag full of bread. Botuk rubs his hands together in excitement. Kysius is looking like a sick puppy. Bron puts up his hands like he is about to start a race, then lets them drop. This was his way of saying, start the story. The night was filled with Kysius telling the boys how he met Lassia and everything they meant to each other. He also told them all the naughty stuff; the breast play in his tent on day one, the threesome at the river with Helda, the spanking he did while fucking her at the river, and her sucking his cock when he was at the river. *Man, I need to go to the river more often.*

The next morning, it was time to fracture the Sacred, load it up, and head home. By the time Kysius woke up from his slumber party, the gemstone was already halfway loaded. He carefully walked up to it, bracing himself for the painful sounds. *Nothing.* It was completely gone. *Oh shit. Did we just kill the first Super Seven in over a century? Please, no. Don't panic. Let's just see what happens when we get home and use the ruby on it.*

He looks down and sees a fractal of the Sacred off to the side, on the ground. *I want to see if I can touch it. I also don't want to die like Lass. Fuck. Her, again. Stop it! Focus!* He very slowly moves his hand over the fractal. As he gets close he only uses his finger tip to tap it quickly, as if he was making sure it wasn't hot. Nothing happened. He got bolder and touched it for longer. Still nothing. He lets out a sigh and grabs the fractal. *Thank God!* Kysius places it in his pocket. He heads back to his tent, while the rest of the gemstone is fractured and loaded. Kysius calls for Espacio to come heal his shoulder. He was done using self-harm as a distraction.

The men have just finished loading the last of the Sacred Seven onto the wagons. It is time to head home. *I have so many memories here. What happens in the midlands, stays in the midlands.* Kysius mounts his horse and joins his friends awaiting him at the rear of the convoy. He doesn't look back as they leave the crash site. Whether it was too painful or just in the past, his eyes only looked forward.

chapter 16
LASSIA

The ladies are finally back in Idyllian territory. Only another day's ride until they arrive at Lass' home. The sun is setting as they enter a small village along their path. Helda sees a sign that reads "Rooms For Rent." They tie up their horses and head inside. Immediately to the right is a freakishly short lady behind a kid-sized counter. The room smelled of cats and tobacco. The decor was very shamanistic. Helda stiffens and grabs a hold of Lassia's hand, who has no situational awareness.

"Hello, ma'am! Hi! We would love to rent one of your rooms," Lass says with a bubbly attitude and smile.

"Twenty coins. You get eight hours. No refunds!" The little lady says with little care and a hint of grumpiness.

"Thank you so much!" Lassia says as she drops twenty-five coins on the counter.

The little lady, absent of expression, hands her a key. Helda and Lassia begin their climb up a very narrow stairwell. Just their luck, a tall skinny man is heading down the steps as they are halfway up them. He is wearing a black cloak, no shirt, and black slacks. By the looks of it, he was not wearing underwear. They awkwardly squeeze against the wall to allow him passage. There isn't enough space and the man accidentally grazes Helda's hip and Lassia's ass with his cock while passing by. *Hello there! That was a nice drive-by.* The ladies let out a giggle as the man retreats down the steps. Helda leads the way to their room. She unlocks the door, and to her surprise, the room is actually decent. It has a large bed, a tall mirror, and a small storage chest at the foot of the bed.

"Wow! Look at us, sleeping in royalty!" Helda says.

"Compared to what we have been sleeping on, absolutely!" Lassia agrees.

Lassia throws herself onto the large bed, face down. Her hair is hanging off the edge. Helda sets their bags down and laughs when she catches a glimpse of Lass.

"Why did he have to be a bad guy? Everything was going so well. I fucking hate him!" Lassia says into the mattress she is face down on.

"You just need a distraction. He is in the past now," Helda suggests.

"I can't shut my brain off. All I can think about is how we had something great and now it's all fucked," Lass complains.

"You have options. You can say fuck it and head up to Ferric to start a new life together or you can come home with me, and I will be your distraction," Helda proposes.

"Bitch, how are you going to distract me? Fucking hand puppets?" Lassia jokes.

"I can use my hands…" Helda says, then bites her lip with a sexy wink. *Ope, my pussy just woke up.*

"Helda! Don't play like that! I am vulnerable," Lass pleads.

"So, you don't want me to distract you like this?" Helda says as she dives her hand between Lassia's legs.

Ooooooohh fuck! Lassia's eyes roll back as she embraces her friend's hand massaging the warmth between her thighs. This is just what Lassia needs right now.

"I think you like this distraction," Helda insinuates.

"Shut up and kiss me!" Lassia demands.

Helda shifts her weight and lunges forward, attacking Lass' mouth like a hungry tiger. Their tongues weave together, competing for entry into each other's mouths. Lassia moves her hand to grab Helda's breast. They moan in unison as her touch makes contact. The other hand is caressing Helda's opposite shoulder. Helda adjusts her hand to go under Lassia's clothes. Her fingers find a wanting pussy with a pool beneath it. Helda penetrates the opening with force.

"Oh fuck! Yes, that feels so good," Lass says in a loud moan.

Lassia arches her back in pleasure and squeezes the bed covers. Helda props herself up and completely removes Lass' pants and underwear. Lassia takes the rest of her clothes off. Helda strips down before lowering her mouth to meet Lassia's legs. She kisses her way up those beautiful long legs. Lassia feels sweet tickles from Helda's lips as she grazes her smooth skin. Finally reaching the core, she laps and sucks on the clit. *Holy shit! I forgot how good she was at this!* Helda lets her tongue explore every inch her friend is offering. She changes speed and intensity, even using different angles to stimulate hard to reach places. Her own pussy is already soaked and aching. Helda can't wait any longer to soothe her own want. She reaches down and rubs her clit, while still devouring Lass'. The level of bliss is so extreme that Lassia's mind is completely blank. She begins to tremble and cramp. *Ooooh myyyy, I am cuuuumingggg.* Helda welcomes the release into her mouth, slowing her actions. *My turn!* Lassia pulls Helda's face to hers for a kiss. Tasting herself in Helda's mouth increases her passion. She pushes Helda down and begins licking and sucking her nipples. Meanwhile, she uses her other hand to pinch and caress the unoccupied one. After a while, she alternates the attention. Knowing her friend must be badly in need of attention between her legs, Lass makes her way down to her friend's cunt. She keeps her hands on Helda's breasts while she makes out with Helda's pussy. As she looks down at a view she never knew she would desire, Helda sees their reflection in the mirror. It is a beautiful sight. For some reason, seeing Lass' hands on her breasts and eating her pussy pushes her to the limit. She lets her orgasm free while watching her reflection. Both women are breathing fast and hard. Not feeling like they had enough, they fall into another kiss. Their hands are frantically roaming each other's bodies. Desperation to feel more consumes them both. At the same time, they reach for each other's openings to put something inside. Their fingers curl and their kissing intensifies. Both women are close to climax. Hot breath crashing as they stop kissing to put more force into their forearms. Moaning and groaning like feral animals, they cum together. This time, it's enough to give them a sense of satisfaction. Helda and Lassia release each other and lay on their backs, beside each other. Catching their breath, the friends simply lay there in peace. Lassia lets out a small giggle. Helda looks over at her and giggles back. That makes Lass start laughing, which of course makes Helda start laughing. Now we have two naked goddesses laughing hysterically after having sex. What a time to be alive!

The sound of a rooster wakes the girls from their beauty sleep. They slowly roll out of bed from being exhausted, for reasons unknown. Helda and Lassia grab their bags and head down the stairs. The little lady is filing her nails. Helda places the room key on the counter. The lady stops filing and gives Helda a death stare. "You girls made quite the ruckus last night. My cats couldn't sleep!"

The ladies look at each other and giggle. The tall man from yesterday walks by them again, in the same outfit. *Yup, still see his bulge.* The little lady is trying to get a look at the gentleman.

"Vee! You owe me rent!" she yells at the lanky man.

"Take a bite, love," he says in a posh accent, as he walks up the steps.

Once again, the girls look at each other and giggle. *Why did that sound so hot? I need help.* They exit the building and ready their horses to continue their journey home. As they head out of town, Lassia feels a sense of hope for the first time since leaving the dig site. She has a great friend and wonderful life to go back to. *Fuck Ky! Who needs him?!*

Reaching the courtyard of her home, Lassia takes a deep breath in and out. Home. She takes a glance at the diamond, majestically displayed in the center. Helda dismounts and begins to unpack the horses. Lassia calls out for Tiger's Eye. He appears from the front door of the fortress. He welcomes her with open arms.

"My sweet Lassia! How was your quest?" Tee asks with a smile that is slowly fading as he realizes the girls are alone.

"We got attacked by Ferric soldiers. They have the Sacred," Lassia says with a worried face.

"Elina will not be pleased. She is already mad that you went on the quest," Tee warns.

"I'd better go talk to her," Lass says with a frown.

"Good luck, little one," Tee offers.

Lassia looks back at Helda and crosses her fingers. Helda reacts with the same gesture. Lass makes her way up the marble stairwell. *Fuck, I am anxious. I am dreading this so much.* She reaches the Goddess' bedroom and knocks. Won't be barging into this room ever again. She hears her step mother beckoning her to come in. Lassia enters to find Elina having her hair brushed by Agate, while Hem is fanning her.

"My baby girl! I missed you!" Elina says, reaching her arms out.

"Missed you, too!" Lassia responds, walking towards Elina to give her a hug.

"So, tell me. How is the Sacred? Did you leave it in the courtyard or did you take it straight to the vault?" Elina inquires.

"Umm, neither?" Lassia replies with nervousness in her words.

"Neither?" Elina asks with confusion.

"We don't have it. Ferric attacked us and took it," Lass admits.

"WHAT?!" Elina yells.

"Sorry? They had an entire army and only my friend and I escaped," she says with desperation.

"Not only did you go on this quest against my wishes, but you came back without the Sacred Seven?" Elina inquires with disappointment.

"I am so sorry. There was nothing anyone could do," Lassia pleads.

"Ugh! I guess you are right. Fuck those Ferric fucks! At least you are okay," Elina says.

Lassia feels a weight lift off of her shoulders. *Oh thank fuck. I thought she was going to kill me.*

"You are still on my shit list, Lass," Elina warns.

"I will make it up to you, promise," Lassia says as she leaves the room.

She walks out the front door and helps Helda unpack. As they are unpacking, Lassia looks over at Helda and sees she looks a tad bit sad.

"What's wrong, babe?" Lass asks.

"It's just now hitting me that this is goodbye," Helda admits.

"What? No! You can't get rid of me that easily, bitch!" Lass says with enthusiasm.

"What? Are you going to make me move in with you? If not, I live a bit far from here," Helda remarks.

"Fuck it, why not? We have plenty of room for activities and I could use a live-in bestie. We could be like roommates. I have never had a roommate!" Lassia exclaims.

"Okay, I can stay for a few days. Then I will make a decision. I have a life back in Anuil, you know? My father and my job," Helda replies.

"Fair enough. Oh my god! We are going to have so much fun!" Lass squeals.

The girls laugh as they gather their things to take them inside.

FRACTAL

chapter 17

KYSIUS

People are lining the streets. They are cheering and celebrating the arrival of Prince Kysius and his army with the Sacred Seven in tow. Villagers still had left over fireworks from the Ruby Festival that could be heard popping in the distance. Kysius has his head held high with pride as he rides his steed through the town as the image of perfection. A few ladies in the crowd flash him as he passes by. He graces them with a smile and blows them a kiss. The villagers' faces go from smiles to pale as Botuk walks in the middle of the convoy. Many of them have never seen a troll. Some children even cry in fear. Botuk tries to hide his laughter as they continue their march. Bron is further behind, helping with the wagons full of fractals. The convoy approaches the castle gates. Always good to be home. A happy King Thrasus awaits with his arms wide open. Kysius hops off his horse to give his father an embrace. *I love this old fuck!*

"My son! Triumphant as always! I see you brought more than just the Sacred," the King says as he gestures towards Botuk.

"Yes! This is my friend Botuk. His actual name is fucking ridiculous so we just call him Botuk," Kysius jabs.

Botuk laughs and smacks him with some force on the back, in a playful manner. *Ouch! Dick! I deserve that.* Kysius lets out a laugh. Bron walks up and waves at Thrasus. The King gives him a standoffish look. It slowly turns into a smile. Thrasus laughs and pulls Bron in for a hug. *What the fuck is happening right now?! My father has never even shaken Bron's hand.*

"Come, let us go inside. I had a feast prepared! I want to know all about this quest," Thrasus says joyfully.

Kysius instructs Commander Kruil to put the fractals in the castle's courtyard and to join them at the feast. The men head into the dining area, where King Thrasus is already sitting at the head of the table. Everyone takes their seats and looks around in amusement. Bron had never stepped foot on castle grounds, much less inside the actual castle. Botuk had never been in a village, let alone a castle. Commander Kruil and Kysius were the only ones not acting like tourists. Food starts to come in from the kitchen.

"So, tell me, how did you happen upon this troll? Botik, was it?" Thrasus asks while chewing on a turkey leg.

"It's Botuk, father. We made camp near his dwelling and some mercenaries got scared. So, naturally, I went to kick his ass," Ky says while throwing a wink at Botuk.

"But instead, he walked into my cave with his tail between his legs. Then when I caught him off guard, he sweet talked his way into becoming my friend," Botuk adds.

"You were totally going to rape and kill me, weren't you big guy?" Kysius inquires sarcastically.

"Indubitably," Botuk says with a laugh.

"How exciting! I miss going on quests. Have I told you about the time I went to Idyll during the summer…" Thrasus starts saying but trails off into mumbling.

"Dad. You okay? What time were you going to tell us about?" Kysius asks with a furrowed brow.

"What? What are you talking about? I need more mead!" Thrasus says angrily.

What was that? He doesn't seem like himself. Kysius motions for one of the servants. He whispers something to him and returns to his meal. He keeps a watchful eye on his father for the rest of the feast. The night goes by in a flash. Thrasus insisted that everyone stay the night at the castle. As they retire to their rooms, one by one, Kysius still has his sights set on his father's behavior. He waits until it is only father and son remaining in the hall. Ky makes his way over to his father.

"Alright, Ky. Out with it then. I know you have been eyeballing me all night. What is on your mind, kiddo?" Thrasus concedes.

"What were you going to say earlier, but stopped? It is not like you to not share your anecdotes," Kysius inquires.

"It was inappropriate. It had to do with a troll. I didn't want to offend your new friend," Thrasus replies.

I smell bullshit. Fuck, Lass. Kysius realizes his father won't tell him the truth. Any further pressing would just anger him and ruin the evening. He lets his father be and heads to bed. Kysius opens up his bedroom door to find three naked women, two human and one orc, lying in wait. *Oh shit! All this for me?* Ky smiles and enters the room before closing the door behind him. He removes his vest and makes his way to the bed. As he gets closer, the women start kissing and groping him. The ladies start rubbing his cock over his pants. *Okay, buddy. Time to get up.* His cock is as limp as a dead frog. Kysius reaches his own hand down his pants to try and start the fire himself. *Nothing. What the fuck?* He tries kissing the girls and grabbing their breasts. One of the girls gets on her knees and starts sucking his limp cock to no avail.

"I'm sorry, ladies. I am afraid the mead was too strong tonight," Ky excuses.

The women grab their belongings with a hint of attitude and leave his chambers. *I swear, if this is because of Lassia…Fuck. I miss her so much. No! Not again.* Kysius grunts loudly and falls back on his bed. He hugs a pillow to his chest as he stares at the canopy over his bed. His eyes feel heavy. He drifts off into a dream.

Kysius is dreaming about a future with Lassia. He sees an image of her standing with two beautiful hybrid children, a baby in her arms and the other holding her hand. There is a house behind them, presumably their home. Then, all of a sudden some hooded figures appear and two of them take the children while the other three start raping Lassia. In his dream, Kysius can't move, can't speak, can't look away. He is stuck watching the woman he loves get violated. Ky's trying everything he can to either break the frozen state he is in or wake up. Just when he thought the dream couldn't get worse, the figures begin stabbing her to death. The only thing he can do is watch in agony. The dream finally ends as he is shaken awake by Bron.

"Ky, are you okay? I heard you crying and screaming from across the hall," Bron says with a worried look on his face.

"It was awful, Bron. They took my kids, a..and they r..raped her and stab..stabbed her!" Ky cries out.

"Who? What kids? Who are you talking about?" Bron asks.

"Lassia! I had a dream that we had a family and some fucking assholes took our kids, then raped and killed her," Kysius says, trying to compose himself.

"Oh, Ky. Buddy, that's a terrible nightmare. Are you going to be okay by yourself tonight?" Bron inquires.

"There is no way of knowing," Ky replies.

Bron sits with his friend as he calms down enough to go back to sleep.

Kysius was not known to be an emotional man. This was only the second time Bron has even seen him cry. One thing both those occasions had in common was the women he cared about being hurt. Bron was realizing just how much Lassia meant to Ky. He left his friend to sleep off the adrenaline and went back to his room.

Kysius wakes up after getting a few hours of sleep. *Last night was fucking ass. Why the hell was I dreaming about that shit? I need to get that woman off my mind. There is plenty to keep me busy around here.* He gets up and makes his way to the dining hall, where his friends are already sitting. Kysius doesn't say a word and takes a seat. They eat their breakfast in weird silence. *Did everyone hear me last night?* He tries to not think too much into it before getting up from the table and heading to the courtyard. The Sacred Seven was still broken into fractals in the wagons. As he reaches the courtyard, he notices his father already skimming the wagons.

"Good morning, Boy-o," Thrasus says.

"Morning, Dad. What do you think about the Sacred? It's quite the sight, huh?" Ky asks.

"I am speechless. The beauty and quality is unparalleled," Thrasus replies.

"It was even more incredible when it was all in one piece. We need the ruby to meld it back together," Kysius explains with a smaller fractal in his hand.

"I am looking forward to seeing it in all its glory," Thrasus admits.

Kysius absently nods as he inspects the fractal in his hand. Thrasus moves beside him and leans in to say something.

"I heard you last night. Everything okay?" Thrasus inquires.

"I just had a nightmare. There's a lot on my mind," Ky admits.

"Did something happen during the quest? The last time I heard you cry like that was when you were a child and I said you couldn't keep goats in your room," Thrasus says with a small chuckle.

"Nah. I think I just had too much mead last night," Kysius lies.

Thrasus knows something is wrong and his son is lying to him. He decides to not press the issue and leaves to grab the ruby. Kysius waits for his father to be out of sight before he places the fractal down and stares at the pile in front of him. *I don't know if I want to live this life without her. No matter what I do, she is all I can think about.* He hears footsteps approaching and quickly grabs the small fractal again, to hide his contemplation.

"Hey bro, what are you up to?" Bron asks.

"Just waiting on the old man to bring the ruby so we can meld this

Sacred back together," Ky replies.

"Got Lassia on the brain, huh?" Bron inquires with a grin.

"What? How did you…?" Ky asks with a raised brow.

"I know you, dude. What are you going to do about it?" Bron asks.

"Nothing. She doesn't want me, bro. I just need to focus on getting this Sacred back together and help my father boost our gemstones," Ky says with determination.

"Fuck that! Let's just go get her. You, me, and Botuk. We go to Idyll and get you that family you dreamed about, minus the rape and murder. Botuk and I will fuck up any figures that pop up," Bron suggests.

I actually love the idea but I can't just leave. My father needs me.

"Let me think about it. Thank you for always being there for me, Bron. I love you, brother," Ky says

"I love you, too, bro. I would do anything for you. Anything," Bron says with a wink.

Kysius and Bron laugh, breaking the tension from the weighted conversation. Thrasus appears from behind a corner. Kysius and Bron fall silent.

"You should go, Ky. I can handle the Sacred Seven. Go get this girl that clearly has your heart. Trust an old man. Every second counts, when you are with the woman you love. You never know when it's the last one," Thrasus urges with pools in his eyes.

Kysius runs over and embraces his father. Both men are feeling the sting of Kya's memory. As they end their embrace, Thrasus places his hand on his son's shoulder and gives him a nod of approval. Kysius returns the nod and takes his leave, with Bron in tow. They grab Botuk, who was playing with some village kids. Children seemed to get over their fear and turned Botuk into a jungle gym. The look of joy on the troll's face was priceless, as he was finally experiencing humans and orc's in a good light. The trio grabs some supplies and prepares to head down to Idyll.

"No matter what happens, thank you guys," Kysius says.

There is a storm on the horizon, as the trio is approaching the Goddess's fortress. The men are exhausted from their long journey. They run into some soldiers standing guard at the gate. Their eyes go wide as they see a large troll holding a club. Botuk smiles at them, trying to ease their fear, but instead it makes the soldiers feel more fear. Kysius raises his hand to draw the soldier's attention.

"Greetings, friends. I am here to see Princess Lassia. Please excuse my friend. He is just excited to be here," Ky says with a smile.

"What is your name? Is she expecting you?" one of the soldiers asks.

"I am Prince Kysius of Ferric. She is not expecting me. I am here to surprise her. So, I would love it if you could keep this between us," Ky pleads.

"We can't let you through," the soldier starts to say.

Botuk lifts his club and places it over his shoulder and gives the soldier a raised brow. The soldier visibly swallows and rethinks his response. Kysius wears a sly smile at the sight.

"Y…you are free to enter. Just don't let anyone know we let you in," the soldier nervously requests.

"Much obliged. Don't worry. We just won't get caught," Ky replies.

The soldiers move aside and allow the men to ride through. They continue their mission to get to the princess. The road is lined with beautiful, tall trees. This place is an oasis. It's gorgeous! They approach the courtyard, where the diamond is on display.

"They just keep their gemstone out in the open?" Bron remarks.

"There is definitely a shield around that bitch. Do not touch it!" Kysius warns.

"Got it," Bron replies.

As they marvel at the diamond, Kysius senses something watching them. He scans the courtyard, which is surrounded by a lattice covered in vines and flowers. *Hmm, strange.* Botuk walks over to a fountain that is off to the side and splashes water on his face. Bron is still busy admiring the diamond, which is so talked about by travelers that visit his bar. Kysius is still on edge.

"We should get out of here. I need to find Lassia and I don't like us being out in the open," Kysius warns.

The men regroup and head towards the front door of the fortress. Ky gets off his mount and walks up to the door. The door is made of wood, adorned with small gemstones and delicate carvings. *Here goes nothing.* They wait a while, with no response. He knocks again. No response. Botuk shoves Ky out of the way and bangs on the door, incessantly. Kysius smacks his abdomen with the back of his hand, knocking the wind out of the troll.

"Hey! Fuck you, dude!" Botuk says with a laugh

"Fuck me? Fuck you! Are you trying to let the whole fucking village know that we are knocking on this door?" Kysius replies with half a smile.

"Let's just go around back," Bron suggests.

Botuk shrugs and Kysius scoffs. They make their way to a garden, located on the opposite side of the structure. There is a blonde woman gardening. *Lassia?* Kysius holds his breath as he waits for the lady to turn around. *Fuck.*

"Is that her?" Bron asks.

"No, it's not," Ky replies, letting out all the air in his lungs.

"Hey! Lady! Where is the Princess?!" Botuk yells.

This mother fucker… Kysius looks up at Botuk with an annoyed look. Botuk looks down at him with a nervous smile and shrugs.

"U..um, I…I don't know," the frightened woman responds.

"Do not fear the troll. He is just excited. He means you no harm," Bron says sweetly.

"O..okay. She might be in her hammock," she says while pointing towards the tree line.

"Thank you, milady," Bron responds with a smile.

"You guys stay here. Lay low. I need to speak to her alone," Ky orders.

Kysius begins his walk towards the tree line. *Please don't hate me. I hope she still has feelings for me. I can't bear being rejected by her.*

FRACTAL

chapter 18
LASSIA

Surrounded by trees, beautiful mushrooms and flowers, Lassia is lounging in her hammock. She has had a great last few days with Helda, who had just left that morning. *I already miss that bitch. Hopefully, she decides to come back and move in. We could take over this whole town together!* Lass daydreams of what life would be like with a partner. Her thoughts turn to a less exciting topic, Kysius. *It's so annoying! We could've had an amazing life together. Ky, Helda and me. Just a happy trio. Raising a family with the love of my life and my best friend. What could be better?* She continued thinking about her fantasy, begrudgingly. Snapping branches interrupt her deep thoughts. She looks over and can't believe her eyes. *Am I still daydreaming?* Kysius is walking towards her with a big smile on his face.

"Hey, Princess. Did you miss me?" Ky asks nervously.

"What? How? Why?" Lass says in shock.

"I can't stop thinking about you. I needed to come see you and earn your forgiveness," Ky replies.

"I can't even sta…" Lass says before her lips are abruptly silenced by Ky's soft lips.

She kisses him back with more intensity than he led with. *What am I doing? Fuck, I missed him!* Their tongues swirl and their lips caress one another. The hot kiss is making them forget the world around them. The moans of sweet desperation and satisfaction are instinctual. Ky's hands roam down to Lass' ass, as he grabs her cheeks and lifts her out of the hammock and pushes her against a tree. Kysius lets out a growl and Lassia moans from the impact. The stormy clouds have reached them. It starts to rain, but it doesn't stop the passionate couple. *I need his cock, now!* She reaches between her legs to stroke his cock over his pants. She feels the full length of his gorgeous cock harden. Her pussy is already wet and ready for him. Lassia slaps him across the face and Ky returns a devilish smile. He puts her down and rips her dress off in one motion. She yelps from the force and the excitement. Ky unsheathes his cock and pushes her shoulders down, forcing Lassia to her knees. Lassia grabs his member with one hand and looks up at him with a submissive look. *Is this what you want?* Kysius sees her beautiful face, ready to do whatever he desires.

"Stick out your tongue," Ky commanded.

She does as he asks. He places his hand behind her head and gently pulls her tongue to his cock. She laps it slowly and methodically. Ky growls with pleasure. She circles the tip of his cock with her tongue and sucks as she goes down the shaft.

"Did you miss this cock, Princess?" Ky asks.

"Very much," Lass replies as she runs her lips along the side of his dick.

He grabs her by the chin and pulls her up. His mouth takes hers with ravenous lust. Without warning, he flips her around and pushes her against the tree. He closes the distance and spits on his cock, for good measure. Lassia is rocking back and forth in anticipation. He spanks her on the ass, with force, making her jolt. He then grabs his cock and rubs her beautiful hole with the tip. She moans with desperation. He spits one more time before putting all his weight behind his thrust. *Oh my god, he is in my ass! Fuck! It feels so big. It feels so full.* Ky is thrusting in rapid succession while spanking her after every few thrusts. Lassia's breasts are starting to feel sore from being pressed up against a tree. Her legs begin to shake. Ky notices she is getting close and wraps one of his arms around her waist and places two fingers inside of her wet opening. He grasps her neck with his free hand. *I am cumming!* She tenses up and creams all over his fingers. Kysius doesn't stop thrusting. Instead, he pulls his fingers out of her and rubs her clit in circles. *He is so good at that.* She feels another wave coming. Ky pauses for a moment and lays down on the ground.

"Ride me, with your ass," Ky demands.

"Yes, Daddy," Lass replies.

She stands over his throbbing cock and sits on it as she moans through every inch entering her. She grinds front to back and up and down, doing anything she could with her body. He is getting close. Ky's balls creep up and she puts her movements into overdrive. It sends him into another dimension as he explodes inside her ass. Feeling his warm seed fill her ass pushes her to the edge, also. She slows her movements to ride out both of their orgasms. They are both breathing hot and heavy. His cock slides out of her and she lays beside him. They fall into the same position they were in during their stargazing date. That was intense! Now they lay there exhausted and satisfied with one big question left to answer. What now?

"Well, that was crazy!" Lassia says, catching her breath.

"I know. That's why I came back for you. I love you! I never want to be without you or this," Ky admits.

"But what about the Sacred? Our parents? How do we make a life together when we are from two completely different worlds?" Lassia asks.

"First off, fuck the Sacred. It's just a trophy. Secondly, our parents will have to deal. Lastly, we can make our own world, Lass. We can find a place to make our own or leave Erythem and search for a new home," Kysius replies.

"How do you sound so sure about everything? Aren't you even the smallest bit worried about any of this going wrong?" Lass inquires.

"Life's too short. I know what I want. I want you and I will do whatever it takes to make you happy. You are my number one priority, forever and always, from this point on," Ky professes.

"I am just supposed to trust you after what you pulled at the crash site?" Lassia asks.

"I warned you and got you to safety before the inevitable happened. Nothing that happened between us was a lie. You know it's true," Ky pleads.

Her eyes lock onto his. She stares deep into the depths of his soul, searching for any sign of a lie or malice. There is nothing but love and adoration looking back at her. Lassia props herself up, high enough for her lips to meet his. She lands a soft kiss.

"Okay. Fuck it. Let's do it. But I have one condition," Lass says.

"Anything," Kysius says with excitement boiling under the surface.

"I get to bring Helda, anywhere we go," Lass requests.

"Oh, fuck yea! Done. I love that bitch!" Kysius says with a chuckle.

"Me too," Lassia says with a giggle.

Kysius gets up and starts getting dressed. Lassia is trying to salvage what she can from her ripped dress.

"One more thing, Ky. You need to talk to the Goddess and get some closure," Lassia demands.

"Fuck, okay. That is probably the smart thing to do," Kysius replies with a frown.

Lassia heads up to her room for some fresh clothes and Kysius goes to find his friends and tell them the good news. *Oh my god, oh my god, oh my god, I can't believe this is happening! I need to get a message to Helda. This is so crazy!* Lassia gets to her room and puts on a new dress. She freshens up with some warm, wet towels and puts on some perfume. *Why not?* She starts laying things out on her bed, in preparation to pack a bag, when Elina walks in.

"Hello, darling. What is all this for?" Elina asks.

"Okay, so I forgot to tell you something that happened at the Sacred Seven crash site," Lassia admits.

"Go on," Elina replies.

"I met the Prince of Ferric, Kysius. And we sort of fell in love. I didn't know he was the Prince until after he revived me with my malachite and I interrogated him. But then he warned me about the army coming and that's how I was able to escape with Helda," Lassia rambles on.

"Wait, what? When did you die and how?" Elina asks.

"I touched the Sacred and it sent so much power through me that it killed me," Lass responds.

"And this Prince brought you back using your malachite?" Elina questioned.

"Mhmm. He has a tourmaline. He is very skilled, in more ways than one," Lassia says with a sly smile.

"Okay, calm down, little girl," Elina cautions.

"He is here, now. He couldn't stand to be away from me. Honestly, I missed the fuck out of him too. Even if he kind've betrayed me," Lass admits.

"Love is a tricky mistress. Trust me, I know," the Goddess says with a raised brow.

"You are talking about Tee, aren't you?" Lass says with a devilish grin.

"Shhh! I don't know what you are talking about!" Elina snaps.

"Okay, nevermind," Lassia says, rolling her eyes.

"I will be in my chambers. I would like to meet this Kysius," Elina says.

"He wants to talk to you, too. I will bring him to you," Lass replies.

Elina nods and makes her exit. Lassia falls back onto her bed with a big sigh of happiness. *This day can't get any better.*

CHAPTER 19

KYSIUS

Botuk, Bron, and Kysius are talking about their options for a new home as they wait in the courtyard for Lassia to escort Kysius to Goddess Elina. The trio is convinced that leaving the continent is the best option. They are all ready for adventure and exploration as a family. *I can just see us now. On a boat, sailing to a new and distant land.* Lassia opens the front doors, wearing a beautiful lavender sundress. Her cleavage is showing just enough. Her hair is waved and worn in a very regal style. All three men's jaws drop. She is a fucking vision.

"Damn, Ky! You never said you fell for an angel," Bron says with enthusiasm.

"She even makes me question my sexuality," Botuk jokes, sort of.

"Easy boys. She is all mine. Maybe I will share after we get off this rock," Kysius says with a devious wink.

How fun would it be to have me and Bron do a spit roast with her? My dick clearly likes the idea. He feels some movement in his nether region. She reaches Kysius and his friends with a big smile on her face. Her eyes are fixated on Ky's.

"She is ready to see you now, babe. I am going to call you babe, from now on. Okay?" Lassia dictates.

"Whatever you want, Princess," Ky replies.

"You boys get to hang out with me. I need to get to know my new family," Lassia says with excitement.

"Oh boy. I like her already, Ky!" Bron yells to an already farther away Kysius.

"I will keep him in check," Botuk yells, insinuating Bron needs a babysitter.

Kysius is walking up the marble stairwell with a mixture of emotions coursing through his veins. He is trying to remember everything he can about his mother's incident and death. At the same time, he is nervous to meet the only family Lassia has left. *Do I come in hot with accusations or get approval as the new boyfriend, first? Fuck! I really hope I don't have to kill Lass' mother. Ugh, stepmother.* He laughs quietly at himself for mocking Lassia's correction. He reaches a door that he thinks is the Goddess' chambers. He knocks. A deep voice yells out for him to enter.

"Welcome, Kysius. I am Tiger's Eye, the Goddess' hand," Tee announces.

"Thank you, Tiger's Eye. Lassia has told me many great things about you," Ky replies.

"Hmm. The Goddess is ready for you, just beyond the partition," Tee directs with a look of disapproval.

Kysius nods and proceeds to his meeting with Goddess Elina. As he reaches beyond the partition, he finally lays eyes on the Goddess. She has Agate, Hem, and Lab at her side, while she is sitting in a lounge chair. *She has more bodyguards than our ruby.* He approaches her and bows.

"There is no need for that, Kysius. You are true royalty. I need to bow to you," Elina says.

"Not at all, Goddess. Let's just skip the awkward customs and courtesies. I never cared for them. Much prefer to be treated like a normal person," Ky admits.

"Very well. You may call me Elina," she replies.

"Okay, Elina. Nice to meet you," Ky smiles.

All three of her servants look at each other in disbelief. They notice her glare and quickly regain their bearing. She brings her eyes back to Ky. She smiles. "So, tell me, Kysius, are you in love with my daughter?" She keeps focusing her eyes on him.

"Yes ma'am. Very much so," Ky admits.

"Do you intend to take my daughter away from me?" Elina inquires.

"I will do whatever makes her happy. That is all I care about," Ky replies.

"Good. I like you already," Elina says leaning back in her chair. "Did you have anything you wanted to ask me? Her hand in marriage? Barter for the Sacred?" Elina inquires.

Kysius laughs for a moment as he realizes she is expecting him to trade the Sacred for Lassia. *I could be wrong, but that would be funny as fuck. Although, I would definitely trade the Sacred for Lassia in a heartbeat.*

"Actually, Elina, I have a question about my mother," Kysius asks.

Agate, Hem, and Lab tense up at the mention. The Goddess may be in danger if this conversation doesn't go well. Their hands slowly make their way to a more prepared position if an attack needs to be defended against. *I see these dickheads getting squirrelly. She definitely knows something. I fucking knew it!*

"Your mother? What would I know about Kya? I only met her once during my last trip to Ferric. God, that was over a decade ago," Elina says with surprise in her voice.

"Do you know how she died? Did you not receive numerous messengers from my father, demanding justice?" Kysius inquires with frustration.

"Justice? For what? How did she die? Kysius, I am sorry, but I am lost," Elina responds with furrowed brows.

"She was raped and murdered by three men in the midlands. The men were said to be from Idyll," Kysius bites back.

"Oh my god! I am so sorry, Kysius. I had no idea. I never received any messengers," Elina replies with tears stinging her eyes.

She is crying?! What the fuck?! She actually didn't know. Well, fuck. Kysius runs his fingers through his hair and lets out a sigh. He is at a dead end in the search for his mother's attackers.

"I believe you. This sucks. So much for closure," Kysius says with exhaustion in his voice.

"No! I will launch a full investigation into this, immediately," Elina snaps.

"What? Really? You would do that for me?" Ky inquires.

The Goddess nods. Ky nods back. The Goddess stands up and Kysius starts making his way out of her chambers. She catches up to him.

"You are a good man, Kysius. You are so much like your father. Don't let him steer you down the same path he took. Make your own," Elina pleads.

"How well do you know my father? I thought you didn't really know each other," Ky says.

"It is ancient history. We had our time together before Kya. It was a wonderful summer. One day he was given a choice by his father between greed and love. He chose greed. Luckily, he met Kya the following week and had you but he was never the same Thrasus," Elina admits.

"He never told me abo…" Kysius says before realizing that's what his father almost said at the banquet.

"It doesn't surprise me," Elina replies.

"You haven't seen him since that summer?" Ky asks while trying to grasp the situation.

"Occasionally, for diplomatic reasons," Elina replies.

"When was the last time you fucked? And don't bother lying. I can smell lies," Ky demands.

"Are you sure you want to know?" Elina urges.

"Absolutely," Ky responds.

"The last time was just before your mother died. After that, I didn't hear from him," Elina says before her eyes widen.

"That is quite the coincidence, isn't it, Goddess?" Ky asks.

"I swear to you, I had nothing to do with it. The timing is peculiar," Elina pleads.

Kysius eyes the men beside her that look even more on edge. *What the fuck is their deal?* Thunder booms and rattles the walls.

"What does it entail to be in the Goddess' service? Are they just bodyguards?" Ky asks.

"They protect and serve me. In all the ways a woman needs," Elina says and gives Ky a devilish wink. "They have been my servants for almost fifteen years. They started at eighteen years of age."

"Interesting. Would you say they are the jealous type? Having their Goddess fuck an Orc king during the occasional diplomatic quest?" Ky asks.

"Are you insinuating that my boys killed your mother?" Elina asks.

"They have been tensing up ever since I mentioned her. They know exactly who I am and what happened. Three teenage boys fall in love with their Goddess and get jealous of her fuck buddy. Instead of going after him like men, they go after an innocent woman picking berries in the midlands," Ky says as his body tenses and readies for a physical altercation.

"Boys. What do you have to say for yourselves?" Elina says with a look of disbelief on her face.

"Okay! Fine! We fucked the Orc King's wife! It was meant to just be a message. We didn't mean to kill her. Lab put mint on his cock and she had a reaction. We panicked and ran away," Hematite admits with defeat on his face.

"Hem! You mother fucker!" Lab yells and cuts his throat.

Elina gasps and backs away in horror. Kysius grows infuriated and charges at Lab. The knife goes flying out of Lab's hand. Kysius is pounding the servant's face in without remorse. He is seeing red to the point that he doesn't realize that Agate is now holding the knife and walking towards him.

"No, Agate!" Elina yells.

Tee hears the commotion and runs to tackle Agate. Kysius is still unloading on Lab's limp body before he feels a sharp pain in his back. *Ow! What the fuck?! I feel cold all of a sudden.* He collapses. Tee is too late. Agate has stabbed Ky in the back. Tee manages to subdue Agate and Elina runs to get Lassia. The ladies return to find Agate tied up in the corner of the room and Tee holding a fading Kysius.

"Oh my god! Babe!" Lassia says with her eyes beginning to pool.

She grabs her malachite and begins to heal his wound. There are many factors that affect a person's healing: blood loss, time since injury, healer's power, and overall health before injury. This type of injury depended on all of it. The depth and placement were not ideal for a healer and the blood loss was not looking promising.

"My malachite is not strong enough. Fuck!" Lass screams in desperation.

She pauses for a second to think. Lass runs out of the room. She comes back moments later with Bron.

"I need you to grab your ruby fractal and do exactly as I tell you," Lass instructs.

Bron is in shock, staring at his dead brother in a pool of blood.

"Bron! Focus! We need to work together to bring him back, okay? Trust me!" Lass screams.

"Okay! What should I do?" Bron asks.

"Grab your fractal, close your eyes, and hold my hand. I need you to will the power of the ruby into my hand," Lass explains.

"I will try," Bron says while sniffling.

"No, Bron! There is no try. There is only do and do not. I need you to do!" Lass bites back.

She puts her malachite in the same hand that is holding Bron's. Using his ruby power to supercharge her malachite. She starts her healing process again. An aura of green and red light is surrounding Kysius' body.

"Is it working?" Elina asks.

"I am so close! I need more power," Lass replies.

Elina runs out to the courtyard where the storm is at its peak. She sees Botuk and stops dead in her tracks. "Oh my god!"

"I am Kysius' friend. I mean no harm. Is he almost done in there? I am getting hungry," Botuk says with a smile.

"He needs my help and I need your help," Elina says frantically.

"What can I do?" Botuk offers.

"I am going to bring the diamond shield down. I need you to smash the diamond so I can get a fractal from it," Elina explains.

Botuk nods and swings his club over his shoulder. Elina moves to the diamond and removes the shield. She gestures to the troll to take a swing. His mighty swing cracks the diamond, but not enough to get a fractal loose. He swings again and more cracks appear. Botuk takes a deep breath and puts both hands on his club. His next swing fractures the diamond into thousands of pieces.

"Yes! Good job! Thank you…er..troll!" Elina says awkwardly as she grabs the largest fractal she can carry in one hand.

"It's Botuk!" Botuk says with a smile as he sways back and forth, having made yet another new friend.

The Goddess rushes back into the room, fractal in hand. She stands between Bron and Lassia and places her hand with the fractal with theirs. Lass is starting to shake from all the power she is trying to channel. Suddenly, everything stops. The aura is gone; Lassia falls to her knees from exhaustion and all three gemstones fall to the floor. Kysius is still not moving.

CHAPTER 20
LASSIA

I failed. He is gone. Everyone is staring at Ky's lifeless body as Lassia is sobbing over him. Bron is frozen in disbelief that his friend is gone. Tee is holding Elina as she processes everything that just happened.

"I need to take him home. Thrasus is going to be furious. I don't know what I am going to do. He is my brother," Bron says with streams from his eyes.

"I will go with you. This is my fault," Lass responds.

"No! Don't any of you blame yourselves for this," Elina demands.

Lassia's tears are all over Kysius. She is caressing his hair and kissing his barely warm lips. No one can take her away from him. Lassia wants to soak up every last second of his presence, while it still has warmth to it. *I am not leaving you. I am right here. I will live the life you dreamed for us. You will always be with me. Everyone will remember the great Prince of Ferric, Kysius.* The emotions spill over her and she begins to sob again. Bron walks out of the room, unable to bear the sight anymore. Everyone else leaves the room, giving Lassia some privacy. She repeatedly tells him she loves him and that it's okay. She tells him to wait for her. Lassia begins to stand up when she feels a hand grab her wrist.

"I'd rather not wait," Kysius says weakly.

"Ky!" Lassia lunges onto him, causing him to groan in pain.

She hugs him so hard it makes her own ribs hurt, but she doesn't care. Lass showers him with kisses. She keeps stopping to hold his face and look into his eyes. *Is this real? Is he really alive? Do I have my baby back?*

"Okay, Lass. I love you but you are making it hard to breathe, babe," Ky whispers.

"Oh my god! You called me babe. I thought I would never hear you call me anything ever again. It was killing me thinking that you had said your last words to me and I never realized it. But here you are!" Lass rambles.

"I have plenty more names to call you, don't you worry, baby girl," Ky says with a devilish grin.

"Leave it to you to die and make a sexual innuendo within seconds of coming back to life," Lass says, rolling her eyes.

"I am who I am, Princess," Ky says, shrugging his shoulders.

"We need to go tell everyone the good news," Lass demands.

"Can we just stay here for a second? I just want to hold you," Ky requests.

"Of course. Anything you want, babe," Lass replies with a look of relief on her face.

The lovers spend the next few minutes together in peaceful silence. Every few seconds Lass would check to make sure he was still alive. He would chuckle every time and she would give him a gentle smack in retaliation for the laugh. Enough time being selfish had passed. Lassia stood up and helped her weak prince back to his feet. They walked out of the room to find everyone standing around looking gloomy and defeated.

"Kysius!" Bron yells and runs into his arms.

The brotherly embrace is forceful, full of love and appreciation. Bron has tears stinging his eyes again. Lassia is off to the side getting emotional at the sight. Botuk makes his way over and turns it into a group hug.

"Ha ha, hey buddy," Kysius says quietly to the large brute that is interrupting his moment with Bron.

"I am glad you aren't dead," Botuk says.

"We all are," Elina adds.

Kysius emerges from the hug and approaches the Goddess. He gives her a hug and looks her in the eyes. They look a lot like his eyes. Kysius takes a step back and looks at her face more closely. He didn't really pay too much attention before. She shares a lot of the same features. Elina notices his face changing as he looks at her. Lassia has a look of confusion as they keep looking at each other like puzzles. *What the fuck are those two doing over there?*

"Why do I look so much like you?" Ky asks Elina.

"Because, Ky, Kya was my sister. You are my nephew," Elina smiles.

"What?! How come you didn't tell me earlier?" Ky demands.

"I didn't think it was the right time. You had learned so much about your father. The last thing you needed was another ambush," she admits.

"Fair enough. I guess we have some catching up to do," Ky smiles.

"I'd rather not. Just take care of my daughter and we can go from there," Elina says.

"Step!" Kysius and Lassia say in unison.

Elina rolls her eyes. Botuk and Bron let out a sigh of relief from all the confusion. Kysius and Lassia laugh at how in sync they are.

"I was about to say…" Botuk starts to say.

"Nope. Just no," Bron quiets Botuk.

A silence falls over them as thunder strikes, sounding further away. Kysius looks to the side and notices Agate is chained up and being held by two soldiers. He starts to walk over to him.

"Kysius, wait. I am going to personally take care of him. She was my sister, remember," Elina says.

Kysius sighs and nods.

"You can rest now. Kya's justice has been served," Elina says with a heavy heart.

Kysius turns away and grabs Lassia's hand. They head to her room, with the boys in tow. As they approach the door, they hear a female voice inside. *I know that voice. No fucking way!* Lass opens the door to see Helda sitting on the bed, singing a song while crocheting a blanket.

"Bitch! I thought you went home?" Lass yells as she crashes in with a hug, knocking them both back onto the bed.

"I stopped when I saw the storm. While I was waiting, I realized I don't want to go back to my old life. I like life with you," Helda admits.

"Well, life is about to get more exciting," Lass says while pulling Helda up to show her the three sexy men at her bedroom door.

"Oh my. You can say that again," Helda smiles.

Shit, why is my pussy throbbing right now? Lassia gestures to the boys to come over. She introduces them to Helda. Botuk shows a very obvious interest, using way more raised brows than normal. Bron's eyes keep venturing over to Ky. *I can't tell if he is worried about his friend or in love with him. Either way, I love it.*

"How about you go show Botuk your rock collection?" Lassia says, throwing her a wink.

Helda gets up and takes the troll with her. She hasn't even closed the door yet and Lassia is getting naked.

"What are you doing?" Ky asks in disbelief.

"I want you. Now, more than ever," Lass smiles.

"What about Bron? You want him to watch?" Ky asks with a laugh.

"No, he is joining," Lass says.

Kysius' laughter comes to a dead halt. He looks at Bron whose face shows he is waiting to see Ky's reaction.

"I don't know. I have never been with another guy before and I don't think Bron has either," Ky says.

"Well, either Bron loves you like a brother or is in love with you. Either way, I think he is more than willing to fuck me with you," Lass says.

"Is any of that true, Bron?" Kysius asks with a furrowed brow.

"I love you like a brother, yes. Also, I am gay. I never told you because I thought you would not treat me the same," Bron confesses.

"Bro, I don't care if you are gay! You are my brother and I love you no matter what. You want to fuck her with me or is that not your thing?" Ky asks.

"Not my thing, unless…" Bron replies nervously.

"You want me, don't you?" Ky says with a devilish grin.

"Mhmmm," Bron nods.

Kysius looks over at Lassia and she gives him a nod of approval. He moves over to a chair and takes his clothes off. Ky sits down and motions them both to come. Bron quickly removes his clothes and joins the couple that already has Lassia sucking Ky's cock. Before Bron gets a chance to get on his knees, she latches on to his semi hardened cock. Both these boys have such nice cocks. She alternates between the men's members. Bron is getting very hard, to his surprise. His eyes are fixed on his friend's muscular body and hard cock. Finally, he gets to his knees and takes a turn with Ky's cock in his mouth. Bron has dreamed about this moment for years. He licks and sucks with appreciation. Every bone in his body is soaking this moment in. Kysius is moaning as Lassia joins in on the fun. He has her on one side and Bron on the other. They are going up and down his shaft, taking turns sucking the tip.

"Sit on it," Kysius commands Lassia.

She gets up and straddles him. She lets herself sink onto his cock, while Bron is suckling Ky's balls. Ky grabs her breasts and sucks on her nipples. She moans with pleasure. *I love when he sucks my nipples.* He bites down on her left breast, making her gasp. He chuckles as he sucks on it even harder to alleviate the pain. Bron stands up and positions himself next to them. Kysius grabs Bron's cock and starts to suck it. Bron growls. Lassia's eyes go wide at the sight. *Holy fucking shit! That is the hottest thing I have ever seen.* Ky is doing his best to imitate what he thinks he should do. Bron is not complaining. Lassia is stuck staring at the boys and an orgasm creeps up on her. She releases and creams all over Ky's cock. Her pussy grips Ky's cock making him hornier. Bron is getting close and Lassia wants a turn. Kysius lifts her up and bends her over. He positions her so that her mouth is at Bron's cock and he is behind her. *A fucking spit roast. Yes!* The boys begin thrusting into her, from both ends. Bron's eyes keep wandering over to Ky. The last glance gets him. He cums down Lass' throat. *Mmm delicious!* She is still getting pounded by Ky. She tightens her legs and feels his cock throb more intensely. She knows he is seconds away. Right on queue, he pulls out and she turns to receive his seed. She gets on her knees before him as he cums all over her beautiful face. They all start laughing. Gotta love post cum giggles. They notice the storm has finally passed.

"Perfect timing. We need to get everyone together to talk about the plan," Kysius says.

"What plan?" Lass asks.

"Our future, Princess. We are all starting a new life together, somewhere new," Ky explains.

She smiles and runs into his arms. They share an embrace before leaving to gather everyone. They get to the bottom of the stairwell and luckily, everyone else is already gathered.

"Now that everyone is here, let's talk about Muria!" Ky says with excitement.

Muria is an island said to be similar to Melan, the continent humans came from. All who went looking for it never returned home, which can be a good thing or a bad thing.

"Muria, huh? That does sound like an adventure," Tee replies.

"I have enough information about it to know it's worth trying. Plus, there are plenty of outlying islands that could also work," Bron adds.

"I have a ship ready with a crew and supplies. Just need to get to the midland port," Ky says with certainty.

"If we leave in the next hour, we can sail as early as tomorrow morning," Bron adds.

No one objects to the plan. They all head out to prepare for the journey. An hour has passed and the horses are ready. Lassia and Helda say their goodbyes to Elina and Tee. Kysius gives a nod from his horse. Botuk is waving with an exaggerated smile. Bron is shaking his head while looking at this ridiculous troll. They ride off to the midlands. As they arrive at the port, Botuk notices there is no ship. In fact, there isn't a single soul in the area. This is very strange, considering this is a very popular dock.

"Ummm, Ky. There is nothing here," Botuk says with confusion.

"What?" Ky snaps.

They ride all the way into the small port town. There is no one around and no signs of a ship on the horizon. They check the tavern, the shops, even homes. It is deserted.

"Something doesn't feel right. You guys stay here. I am going to check the north road," Ky mutters.

Kysius doesn't need to get far to find what he feared. Piles of dead, rotting bodies are in front of him all placed in a ditch. He covers his nose and mouth and rides back to his friends.

"We need to leave, now!" Kysius commands.

"Why? What did you find?" Lass asks.

"The illness is here," Ky warns.

The illness is here…

FRACTAL

FRACTAL

ABOUT THE AUTHOR

Daniel Jaws writes for your pleasure. His words and ideas come from your fantasies. He makes your desires his own and molds them into stories. Stories that bring out all of your emotions, even the ones you hide.

FRACTAL

ðear reaðer

Fractal is a love letter. It was a private project that was never meant to be seen by anyone beyond the intended reader. I offer this story to you, my strangers, with the hope that it brings you a sense of enjoyment as the story of Fractal unfolds. Giving my story your time and attention is the highest honor.

-With my deepest gratitude.

Daniel Jaws

P.S. Turn the page

FRACTAL

FRACTAL

Good girl.

www.ingramcontent.com/pod-product-compliance
Lightning Source LLC
Chambersburg PA
CBHW071928220626
47052CB00002B/503

* 9 7 8 1 9 5 6 5 4 4 7 2 5 *